When You Least Expect It

This book is a wo names, characters, places this book are the product of the author's imagination and any resemblance to persons, living or dead, locales or actual events is purely coincidental.

Copyright © by Catherine Scott 2015

All rights reserved. Except as permitted under the U.S. Copyright Act of 1976, no part of this book may be reproduced, distributed or transmitted in any form or by any means, ort stored in a data base or retrieval system, without the prior written permission of the Author.

First eBook edition: April 2015

ISBN: 978-0-9962603-1-2

Cover Design:

Rebel Edit & Design

Catherine Scott

DEDICATION	**5**
PROLOGUE	**7**
Chapter 1:	**8**
The Past and The Future	*8*
Chapter 2:	**15**
Life Changes	*15*
Chapter 3:	**36**
Hitting the Reset	*36*
Chapter 4:	**41**
On the Road to the Future	*41*
Chapter 5:	**54**
Preparation	*54*
Chapter 6:	**62**
Teacher Institute	*62*
Chapter 7:	**76**
First Day of School	*76*
Chapter 8:	**98**
Getting Close	*98*
Chapter 9:	**115**
New Beginnings	*115*
Chapter 10:	**138**
Love	*138*
Chapter 11:	**144**

Changes	*144*
Chapter 12:	**151**
Giving Thanks: Visitors expected and not...	*151*
Chapter 13:	**165**
Just When You Thought Things Were Going Well	*165*
Chapter 14:	**177**
Protective Instincts	*177*
Chapter 15:	**187**
Inspiration	*187*
Chapter 16:	**195**
Turning the Tables	*195*
Chapter 17:	**200**
Waiting	*200*
Chapter 18:	**218**
Normal, or Close Enough	*218*
Epilogue:	**225**
Happily Ever After	*225*
Acknowledgements	**231**
About Catherine Scott	**232**

DEDICATION

To my co-workers, who I'm lucky enough to call friends!

*...things happen when you least expect them.
Things that can change your whole life.*

-Lesley Kagen

PROLOGUE

"Higher! Swing me higher, Daddy." Her nine-year-old self squealed.

"Okay, Okay! But be careful, and hold on tight."

Jade squealed in delight as her legs folded in and out in time with the swing of her body; back and forth, soaring her even higher until suddenly her motion shifted to the side, causing her to lose her balance.

Her father carefully eased her onto her back and called out to another child nearby to run home and call 911. While her father and she waited for the wail of sirens that would indicate help was on the way, he took her hand in his. He gently whispered, "That's life, sweetheart. When you least expect it—well, you end up getting hurt."

CHAPTER 1:

The Past and The Future

Nothing is so painful to the human mind as a great and sudden change.
-Mary Shelley

Jade Davis woke up and shook off the remnants of the dream. This wasn't a day to be sad. Jade was on her way to accomplishing everything she ever planned. It was time to get ready. After a moment, she emerged from her shower and began collecting the clothes she intended to wear under her gown. Jade thought she should wear slacks or a skirt under her graduation robe but she decided against it. Instead, she chose a pair of shorts and a t-shirt, given the unseasonably warm temperatures that she knew were only masked by the air conditioning in her apartment.

Jade checked her reflection in the full-length mirror. After applying powder to cover the freckles on her cheeks and some lip gloss, she was ready to leave. She slipped on a pair of sandals that were a bit dressier than what she would normally choose in deference to the occasion. Her large, dark green eyes looked especially prominent on her pale face.

She looked out of her second floor apartment window and watched as some of her neighbors, who were also graduating, posed for pictures with family members by their cars. It was time, so she left to attend her graduation alone. She could have asked her best friends Nick and Lisa to be there. They had wanted to see her graduate, but it hadn't felt right. This day was for her mother; the milestone they had both planned for. Her eyes were suspiciously moist when she grabbed her wallet and keys, as she headed out of the door.

Jade drove to the campus automatically and couldn't help reflecting on the event that changed everything. She remembered the headline "St. Patrick's Day turns tragic for a mother and daughter after attending Chicago's Annual Parade." Luckily there weren't any pictures released to the media of the accident. However, the media took plenty of pictures of the funeral guests. Reporters couldn't pass up an opportunity to gawk at people in mourning, she thought bitterly.

Her father hadn't shown up for the funeral. After all, he disappeared without as much as a letter or phone call for 10 years. He never even met Sarah, or had the opportunity to find out what a great kid she was.

She thought about the day that her father left. She came home and saw her mother crying. When she'd asked why she was upset, her mother answered with, "some things can't be forgiven." She had then quickly pulled herself together enough to take her out for her favorite fast food dinner. She didn't find out until much later that her father had left for good. The thing that hurt the most was that he never told her goodbye.

Soon after that Jade learned that her mother was pregnant. She expected her father to come back, but he never did. So Jade took care of her mother through a stressful pregnancy, and then her little sister, Sarah. Jade came home right after school every day so that she could do the cooking and tutor students in the evening. By the time she was sixteen; Jade was working nearly full-time as a waitress while attending high school. It was no wonder that she never dated much. Her mom never said anything to her about boys except that, "There will be plenty of time for them later" and,

"Sometimes men can lead to trouble," but she never explained anything more about what she meant.

Jade knew her mother had a box full of letters and pictures that she would go through when she thought Jade and Sarah were asleep. She was curious about them, but Jade never tried to read them. She supposed that that box was a key to an understanding she couldn't face. Some things were better left unknown.

Jade snapped out of her reverie to listen the names of the other college graduates called. As her name's announcement drew closer, she prepared to stand up. She briefly touched her mother's Claddagh ring as she stood to walk to the stage.

At the ceremony, Jade had to admit that she got caught up in the enthusiasm of the day. Even though she hadn't been particularly close to any of her fellow students, Jade found herself absorbed in their fervor exchanging contact information, hugs, and even posing in group photos with classmates she hadn't spent much time with previously.

Jade felt regret seep in as she drove back to her apartment. She realized for the first time what she had missed in her years of virtual isolation. She had spent so much time protecting herself from the outside world and focusing entirely on her school work that she had created an impenetrable barrier from any potential connections besides Nick and Lisa.

Jade recalled the events that had helped her move beyond the immediate grief of her mother and sister's death. For several weeks after their funeral, Jade hadn't gone to work or left the apartment she had shared with her family. Her neighbors came by and brought food and really tried to help her, but she could barely manage to leave her bed. It didn't seem right to go on but ultimately she got tired of her self-imposed isolation.

She realized that she needed to get out of there, so she got out of bed, got herself cleaned up and left the apartment that was smothering her. Once outside, she got in her car and started driving without purpose or direction. After a short drive, she saw an unfamiliar café and decided to stop. She ordered tea and a cookie and was walking to a table when she caught sight of a young woman with long hair and colorful clothes. She was sitting at a corner table with a deck of cards and a sign that read "Tarot Readings." Jade had never believed in psychics or occult phenomena, but she found herself intrigued, so she decided to check it out.

"How much for a reading?

"Full reading is twenty. Answer to a question is ten."

"Well, I don't have a question…just give me a full reading," she said as she took out her wallet.

"My name is Rena. Go ahead and shuffle these cards."

After a few shuffles, Jade placed the cards in front of Rena, who then picked them up and began placing them around the table in front of her in a ten card pattern.

"Well this is interesting. It's a strong reading. You can tell because of all of the major arcana cards which are these cards here; the death card, the fool, the tower and the lovers. The suits are also important; cups represent emotions, wands represent material or financial concerns, pentacles refer to spirituality and swords refer to struggle, and this is you at present—the death card." Jade's face showed shock before Rena quickly added, "Don't take the cards literally. The death card doesn't usually represent physical death. Actually, it's more like the end of a journey, or a change in a way of doing things. It's better if we look at all the cards first, and then try to interpret what they all mean.

Taken as a whole, I would say that you are standing at a crossroads between your old life and your new one and all you need to do is have a little faith. So, even though you didn't ask a question, the cards seemed to have answered you anyway."

Jade nodded her head, trying to maintain her composure even though she could feel the blood rush to her cheeks. Trying for a smile, Jade offered Rena a quiet nod and gave her thanks before walking to another table in a daze to finish drinking her tea and eating her cookie, which now didn't sound very good.

Jade was haunted the rest of the night by Rena's reading. She had been at an impasse—stuck at a crossroads between her old life and moving on. The realization that even though it wouldn't be easy to make a change, she needed to acknowledge that her mother would want her to move on. She had received her mother's life insurance settlement, which brought her to the logical conclusion that her mother and sister wouldn't want her to mourn them indefinitely, especially like this, so she would put the insurance settlement to good use.

After some research, she found that she could go online to schedule an appointment for advisement at the local teacher's college. Within a couple of weeks, she had enrolled and packed up her apartment, cancelled her apartment lease and found a new place to live that was much closer to campus. This was what needed to happen and she was ready for what the future would bring.

CHAPTER 2:

Life Changes

Louie, this is the beginning of a beautiful friendship.
                                                 -Casablanca

Jade's adjustment to life as a student was surprisingly easy. She enjoyed her classes and found that the course work was challenging enough to help distract her from her grief and loneliness but she needed something else. Jade immediately thought about getting a job. She had been working as a waitress since she was a teenager. Working provided her the opportunity to make some spending money and help Jade stave off her loneliness.

"I saw the Help Wanted sign in the window. What type of help do you need?" Jade asked the man at the counter. He had a warm smile and his name tag said his name was Nick.

He considered her for a moment before responding, "I'm looking for a waitress. I need one as soon as possible, but they have to be reliable. I can't take any more chances on high school students."

"Well I'm looking for a job."

"Do you have any experience?"

"Yes. I waitressed all through high school."

Nick smiled and immediately called out to his wife, Lisa, for an application. Jade quickly explained her situation as a college student and her availability. The next thing she knew she was walking out the door with a work schedule written on an index card. She set off for her first class of the day feeling inexplicably lighter.

~~~~ Four Years Later~~~~

"Do you need any help in there, Lisa?" Jade asked when she arrived for a post-graduation celebration dinner with Nick and Lisa.

"No honey. It's a celebration for you so sit yourself down and talk to me while I finish. Nick just went to get some beer." Jade knew better than to argue with Lisa so she sat down and watched her cook.

"Smells wonderful, I love your lasagna but I can't believe you wanted to cook on your day off. You shouldn't have gone to all the trouble," Jade said, pinching off a small piece of garlic bread while Lisa's back was turned.

"I saw that," Lisa said laughing. "Here, put these plates on the table, Beautiful." Jade smiled and laid the plates out around the table and debated trying to pull another piece of bread off before dinner.

"Of course we wanted to do a special dinner for you. I hate that you graduated without anyone there to cheer you on." She said frowning just as Nick walked in. "Honey, back me up," Lisa yelled out, "Don't you think Jade should have let us come to her graduation?"

He walked into the dining room and looked at both of the women now seated at the dinner table and sighed as he put set the beer down and put his hands on Lisa's shoulders.

"Love, it was her decision. She had her own reasons for wanting to go to it by herself. We're her friends and we need to be supportive, even if we don't agree."

"Way to gang up on me! How do you expect me to come up with a solid defense for myself when you have all this wonderful food to distract me?"

"Well that's all part of our evil plan, didn't you know?" Lisa laughed.

"Here," Nick said, "first of all, everyone take a beer and let's make a toast."

Jade smiled and raised the frosty beer mug that Lisa had set out for them, "To toast." She laughed and caught Lisa's attempt at a stern expression and apologized.

"To you, Jade. Congratulations! We love you!"

Jade tried to keep from choking up and stood up to hug both of them quickly. "Now can we eat?" She asked trying to appear unfazed.

"In a second, Nick, honey, where did you put the present?" Oh, never mind. There it is!"

Nick laughed and watched his wife hand Jade the small wrapped box. Jade looked down and her eyes misted up at the kind gesture. As she slowly peeled the purple bow off of the top and tore the iridescent gift paper. She took the top off the box, revealing a small black jewelry box. She slowly opened the hinged box and saw a delicate white gold necklace.

Lisa spoke softly, "It's an anchor necklace. It means you always have a home with us. We love you." Jade's eyes filled up and Lisa quickly rushed in to hug her. "Shh, now honey. Don't cry. Here, let me help you put it on." After she fastened the necklace around Jade's neck she looked at her face, "Please don't be sad. It's a celebration, so let's go have some beer and start eating."

Once everyone had their food, Nick asked Jade about the ceremony, "Well it took forever and it was really hot in the auditorium, but it really was nice. There were a lot of speeches, but they weren't too bad, I guess." She conceded.

"So are you sure you're up for more school? I mean, it seems like you really enjoyed teaching. I'm surprised you don't just do that for a while because you're such a natural with kids." Lisa said. When Jade didn't respond, she continued. "All of your evaluations went so well. Would you really rather be a counselor?" "Honey, do what you want. We just want you to be happy." Nick jumped into the conversation and passed Jade the garlic bread.

"I've been thinking about it, actually. I even looked online at the teaching positions available. I didn't intend to teach so I never went to the job fairs that they had on campus because I was curious what the job market looked like." She felt as if she was betraying her mother's memory by considering changing the plans she helped her make.

As if reading her thoughts, Lisa and Nick exchanged a knowing look. "It's okay to check things out, you know. I know you made plans before, but it's okay to keep your options open—maybe even change your mind."

"I just want you guys to know how much I appreciate you. You're my family."

Nick reached over to pat her hand. "Thanks honey, but it wouldn't hurt to let other people in too."

Nick decided to try and help out in that department. He had learned from his best friend, Al that his younger brother was moving back into the area. He hadn't met Joe before, but it seemed to be great timing. Nick and Lisa wanted Jade to make more friends, hopefully even date, so introducing Jade to the younger brother of his best friend seemed like a great opportunity to help Jade get out there, but he would wait. Tonight was about Jade, and he wanted to make sure she would have a good night with him and Lisa. Tomorrow would be a good time to get the ball rolling.

"Jade? Can you come here for a minute, Sweetie?" Lisa asked the next morning after the breakfast rush was over. When Jade poured herself a diet soda and sat down in front of her. "I want to state right now that this isn't a fix up, ok? But Nick has this friend, Al that served in the Army with…"

Jade interrupted, "Hate to tell you this, but it sounds like a set up to me."

"Really, Sweetie, I just have this friend and his younger brother is new to the area, so I was thinking you guys could meet. No pressure, I swear." Nick assured her.

"Guys, really..." Jade was ready to frame her objections but looked at them both and came up empty. "Oh, alright, I'll meet him, but I make no promises beyond that. Okay?"

Lisa came around the counter and hugged her, "You're the best, and I promise no pressure, but you never know. Don't be so ready to ignore the possibilities. He could turn out to be a great friend, maybe something more. Anything is possible."

Joe fingered the scar on his forehead that his hair now concealed. His fiancée, Diana, had walked out on him when he refused to get counseling, but Joe had had enough of quacks after the accident. No way was he going to lie down on a couch and spill his guts. He lost his job, which he had a right to be angry about it, but then he lost everything else. Someone needed to pay for taking away everything that was his.

He was more than curious when his brother's friend Nick called to invite him over for dinner, and wanted to introduce Joe to a friend of his. He wasn't excited to go at all, but really, he had nothing else to do, so he accepted the invitation and prepared himself to meet with people he could care less about.

They made plans to have brunch at Nick and Lisa's home the following Sunday since the restaurant was closed. Joe arrived first. Jade showed up not long after Joe, coming dressed in jeans and a blouse. She wasn't going out of her way to impress this friend of Nick's, so she didn't have any hopes going into this. Just dinner and then she would be heading home.

He sat in the living room on the couch watching the Cubs game with Nick. She noticed that he was good looking enough, with dark blonde hair and a lean, stocky build. Both men seemed pretty engrossed in the pre-game discussion so she didn't interrupt them, so she joined Lisa in the kitchen.

"What can I do, Lisa?" Jade asked.

"It's all about done, actually. You can set the table, though. I already took the plates out so just put those out with the silverware and these cloth napkins."

"Ooh, fancy cloth napkins." Jade teased. Lisa swatted her good naturedly with a dish towel.

The brunch went well but Joe didn't say much. He never really looked at or appeared interested in Jade.

Whenever Nick or Lisa tried to ask him a question, he replied in one word answers. Just as they were finishing up, Joe was called into work and Jade was quietly pleased. The meal had been incredibly awkward for everyone. Looks aside, she thought for sure that there was not a thing that they would have in common. She was happy that she had dodged that bullet.

'Who would've believed it' Joe thought to himself on his way to work the next morning. His brother's friend Nick tried to set him up with a real babe. Usually when someone set him up, the woman turned out to be a serious dog, but Jade was hot. She had shoulder length, honey blonde hair and a pretty face. She seemed cordial enough, but he got the impression that she was probably a real stuck-up bitch, too good for a guy who really works for a living. Maybe, but Joe could see the possibilities. He got called in before he could ask her out, so he would just stop by the restaurant and find his opportunity. Jade could definitely be a good time under the right circumstances, but she might need to be taken down a peg or two first like his ex, Diana."

A couple of days later, Joe stopped by on his night off and had to wait to sit at one of Jade's tables. 'Apparently, *she's popular,' he* thought. After about 10 minutes, he was seated at a small table next to the kitchen.

"Hi Joe," Jade said with a cautious smile. She handed him a menu and glanced quickly at her other tables.

"Hello, Jade, I'm sorry I had to rush off after dinner. It happens sometimes."

"That's okay," Jade quickly offered, "Can I get you some coffee?"

"Sure, I take it black."

"You got it. I'll be right back."

A few minutes later, after she had poured several more cups of coffee and brought another table their check, she returned to Joe's table with her pen in hand. "What can I get you?"

Joe took a moment to scan her body before he spoke, "I'll have the ham and eggs with an order of wheat toast."

Trying not to shudder at the unwelcome perusal, Jade cheerily responded, "Coming right up!"

Joe's food was delivered by another older waitress and he dug right in. When Jade returned a few minutes later to refill his coffee, he quickly spoke up, "Listen, I was wondering if maybe we could go out sometime. Do you like a good steak?" Joe asked with a cocky grin.

"I'm sorry," Jade answered, "I kind of have a lot going on right now. I'm not really looking to date at the moment."

"Yeah, whatever, it's no big deal." He quickly glanced at his watch and pulled the sports page in front of him. She was relieved to notice the next table beckoning her. Giving one last apologetic smile, she moved on.

"Well that didn't go over too well," Jade muttered under her breath as she walked into the kitchen.

Lisa looked up and asked her, "What didn't go over too well?"

She leaned against the counter and sighed. "Joe just asked me out, but before you jump all over me about it, he was sort of creepy."

Lisa's eyebrows lifted as she used a spatula to move a stack of hotcakes off the grill. "Creepy, how?"

"He gave me a full body scan, like he was imagining me naked. I swear, he gave me the willies!"

"Seriously? Maybe you were just thinking too much into it. I mean, you're very pretty, Jade."

"No," Jade quickly added, "It was really obvious. How well do you know the guy, anyway?"

Lisa answered a bit sheepishly, "Actually, Nick knows his brother really well, but I don't think he ever met Joe before. Honey, don't worry about it. If he makes you uncomfortable, then that's enough for us."

When Jade went back out to the dining room, Joe had already finished eating and left. He had left a twenty on the table that more than covered his meal.

The other waitress caught her puzzled expression and asked, "Everything okay?"

"Sure," she answered, but she couldn't help but feel that maybe it wasn't.

A couple of days later, Joe returned to the restaurant. He'd obviously come in after a day of work and he looked tired, but this time he sat at a table that wasn't in her section. He ate dinner without further incident but every time Jade crossed the room, she felt his eyes following her. Nick was busy doing paperwork in the back room and Lisa was cooking so she just did her best to ignore him.

The following day he came in again, finding a table in her section. He ordered a patty melt plate and a coke. Jade nodded and he pulled his smart phone out of his pocket.

'Okay, that wasn't too bad,' she thought.

When she returned later with his food and a refill on his soda, he politely thanked her and she moved on to wait on other customers. When she returned several minutes later with the bill, Joe reached out to grab her wrist. "I'm really sorry about the other day," he said in a reassuring tone. Jade stared first at his hand on her wrist and then at him with an angry expression on her face. His expression quickly turned nasty as he pulled away from her, "Oh, I get it. You're a little princess. You're one of those who think they're too good for a guy who actually works for a living. I guess you're type is looking for a surgeon, or someone who makes a lot of money, huh?" Joe said, his face turning red with anger.

Before Jade could respond, Nick put his hand on her shoulder and considered Joe wearily. "Problem here?"

"Nope. No problem," Joe said, looking from Nick to Jade, "Oh, so that's how it is, huh."

Nick's face turned red, but before he could respond to Joe's bizarre comment, Lisa interrupted, "Joe, don't worry about the bill. It's on the house, but it might be better for everyone if you eat somewhere else from now on, okay?"

"Sure, whatever, it's not like the food is that great." Jade noticed Nick's fists curl up at his sides but luckily Joe took the hint and walked out without further comment.

The next day, Jade left the restaurant after her shift and drove straight to her favorite forest preserve to take a walk. There was nothing like walking through the trees to help you think without the chatter and background music. She had already changed her clothes and tennis shoes, and when she locked her car, it occurred to her for a moment that most people wouldn't feel like going for a walk after six hours on their feet, but the truth was that she hadn't slept well the night before. Jade had dreamt about the incident the night before with Joe. She just didn't understand why a stranger would act so bizarrely towards her. A part of her felt a little guilty, but that didn't really make sense. It's not as though she had done anything wrong. She tried to be straightforward with him and honest as to why she didn't want to go out with him. She thought he'd understand that.

She was so lost in thought that she didn't notice him parked, watching her as she entered the trail.

Jade had been about to finish her evening shift at the restaurant when Joe walked in with a single red rose.

Nick had been talking to a couple of regulars at the counter when Lisa motioned over to him. He quickly stopped talking when he noticed Joe, then he glanced across the dining room for Jade. He quickly rounded the counter and crossed the room in two long strides. "Joe, what are you doing here?"

Joe looked at him with a sheepish expression. "I just wanted to apologize for my outburst the other day. Can I talk to Jade?" Nick motioned for him to come over to the register.

At that moment, Jade registered Joe's presence. She quickly went to the kitchen and Lisa followed. He tried to call out to her but Nick spoke to him before he got any words out. Nick spoke in a calm voice, "I'm sorry Joe, but Jade is really not interested. I think you scared her."

Joe immediately looked concerned, "I don't understand why she would be afraid of me? I just asked her out for dinner. What was scary about that?"

Nick spoke to Joe quietly, for the first time realizing just how unbalanced he was. "Well you said some other things, Joe...and well, they seemed strange."

Joe's face turned red and he started to protest but at that moment, two policemen walked in. They seated themselves at the counter and called out to Lisa in the kitchen. Buzz and Carl were both regulars, but Joe didn't know that. He seemed to reconsider what he was going to say and quickly said, "Never mind. I wasn't trying to cause any problems," then muttered something about the rose being for Jade and walked out of the small restaurant without looking back. Nick took a deep breath after Joe left and quickly slapped both officers on the back and announced to them both, "Dinner is on me guys!"

For the next week, Jade felt on edge. She hadn't seen Joe again, but she couldn't shake the uneasy feeling she had. Nick seemed to share Jade's concerns because he insisted on walking her to her car after each shift. Nick received an unexpected delivery one evening, so Jade decided not to wait for him. When she got to her car and opened her door, a single red rose lay on her seat. Jade opened her mouth to scream but the sound died in her throat when she felt a hand clutch her shoulder from behind. Jade swung reflexively around and smashed Nick in the face with the heel of her palm.

"Oh my God Nick, are you okay? You scared me to death."

"I guess I didn't have to be so worried about you, Sweetie. I think you broke my nose."

"Here, let me help you up. We need to get you some ice, and don't lean your head back. Jesus, you're bleeding all over."

"Of course I am. Damn girl, I saw stars. If you don't mind, I'm going to tell people I got mugged in the parking lot."

Jade held the rear door open for the restaurant. Lisa saw them just as Jade helped Nick into the kitchen, "What in the world happened?" Lisa asked as she grabbed a clean rag to put on his nose.

"Honey, we don't have to worry about Jade. She clocked me."

Lisa stared at Jade.

"He snuck up on me!"

Lisa gave Nick a dirty look. "Hasn't she been through enough?"

"Hey, I'm injured. Give me a break."

"Why did you get so freaked out, anyway? I know I startled you, but..."

"That guy, Joe. He left a rose in my car. I mean, the car was locked. How could he get in?"

"He's an electrician sot probably wasn't that difficult. I think it's time to call the police." Jade agreed and made the call while Lisa attended to Nick's bloody nose.

After Jade talked to the police and filed a report, Nick and Lisa insisted that she stay at their house for the night. Jade agreed and stayed in their spare room, but she couldn't sleep. "Crap, what am I going to do?" Jade thought aloud, her heart racing. Resigned to a restless night, she stared up at the ceiling while sleep never came.

The next day, Nick and Lisa drove Jade to the police station to file for a restraining order. The police were sympathetic but honest with her. "If he comes to you again and you call us, we'll arrest him, but that might not do you much good."

"What do you mean? I thought the restraining order would help keep him away from me."

Lt. Danielle O'Malley looked at her apologetically, "Well we have to catch him in the act of trying to approach you. We can charge him if we catch him violating the restraining order but…well honestly, if he breaks into your house or catches you alone, a piece of paper isn't really much protection."

"Seriously? Then what's the point of filing this then?" Jade asked.

"I know it doesn't make sense. The laws regarding stalking aren't very effective. I know it's frustrating, but maybe he isn't really dangerous. I hope for your sake he isn't. I'm going to give you my card, and if you need anything, just give me a call. My cell number is on there too."

Jade took the card and thanked her. She drove her car home but kept it locked until she scanned the area around her apartment building. Jade ran uneasily from her car into her apartment building and texted Lisa about what the police had said. Lisa texted back that she and Nick would stop by after the restaurant closed. While she waited for them, she decided to check her email.

Jade barely registered anything in her inbox at first. She immediately sent most of it to the delete folder, but then one message caught her eye. Teachers urgently needed in the Southern part of the state, 'click the link' to reply, so she did. A small rural school district in the southern part of the state was seeking a special education teacher. She quickly sent her resume and application off electronically and went to bake a batch of chocolate chip cookies for Nick and Lisa.

When they stopped by Nick and Lisa didn't seem to know what to say about Joe except how sorry they were about trying to fix her up with him. Nick had emailed his friend to ask if he knew anything but him being in the military, it often took awhile to respond.

"It's not your fault. You were trying to be good friends because you don't want to see me alone." She then took a deep breath and told them about the application she had just submitted. "I'm not sure why, but it felt like the right thing to do. I mean, I might not even get a response."

"Of course you will."

"I'm putting it in the hands of fate. Best case scenario is that I get a teaching job three hundred and fifty miles away. The worst case scenario is that I'm working on my masters' degree and possibly being stalked. We'll see how it all turns out, I guess."

The response to her application came the next afternoon. She got a phone call from the building principal expressing their interest in her application and two days later, she had a Skype interview.

The interview with the principal went well. Apparently, the former teacher's husband had received a transfer out of the area, so they were in dire need of a replacement. The school principal offered Jade the position and gave her a couple of days to think it over. Jade was told that they would have to get the hiring approved by the district's Board of Education, but asked if she could come down to take part in some training in the middle of July. That gave her three weeks to withdraw from her graduate program, find a place to live near Nairobi, pack her apartment, and say goodbye to Nick and Lisa.

Jade found a small house that was available for rent with an option to buy, basis ten minutes away from the school. She had to buy new furniture since most of the pieces she had weren't worth the cost of hiring a moving truck for, so she donated almost everything in her apartment and sold the rest. As a result, Jade was able to pack all of her belongings which consisted of her clothes, books, framed pictures and other assorted mementos in the back of her small sedan.

Jade said, willing herself not to cry, "I'll come to visit on school breaks. It's all going to work out, I promise."

They both nodded their heads and grabbed her in a tight hug. Jade managed to make it onto the highway before she let the tears fall. She turned the 80's music on her radio up loud and sang along, just before she said to no one, "And now for something completely different."

CHAPTER 3:

Hitting the Reset

Sometimes the hardest part isn't letting go, but rather learning to start over.
-Nicole Sobon

The drive southward toward Nairobi, Illinois seemed to take forever. Northern Illinois' flat and characterless roadsides offered nothing of interest. Central Illinois' farmlands provided endless miles of grain fields, advertisements for rest stop fast food, and various brand name fertilizers. It wasn't a particularly attractive drive until she neared Effingham, and at that point, the landscape became more varied foliage and topography. When she finally reached Nairobi, it was late afternoon and the July evening was still steeped in bright sunlight. However, she wasn't prepared for the obvious desperate economic state of the town.

She had heard that unemployment was high in the area, and that was certainly evident as many buildings were worn or torn down, and those that were still standing revealed little character in the far southern Illinoisan city. Jade had a moment of worry that she wasn't up to teaching in this town until she met with the principal, Mr. Jameson.

He explained that Nairobi had once been a much more prosperous city, where people once came to shop in the large department stores. There were once movie theaters, night clubs, etc., but in the 1960's, Nairobi struggled with racial discord and many people fled, which caused many businesses to close along with them. Since then the town struggled with the same issues as other small rural towns; high unemployment, generational poverty, and shrinking infrastructure. But instead of sounding depressed about it, he sounded optimistic.

"The good thing about being down and out is that there is no place to go but up."

"I can definitely get on board with that." Jade said, liking the hope in his words.

Mr. Jameson smiled and then went on to explain the training that she needed to undergo. He explained to her that the district wanted her to attend a reading conference in New Orleans in a week with the language arts teacher, Ms. Lewin.

Rose Lewin was a petite, curvy redhead with black framed glasses who seemed eager to meet Jade. Jade hardly had the chance to speak as Rose started explaining the details about the conference. They were set to share a room and would drive together. Rose told Jade what the conference had been like the year before, then showed her around her classroom, including her endless bulletin board of photos. She rattled off student names and stories Jade would never be able to remember. Before Jade left, her head was spinning, but she had Rose's contact information and a copy of the conference flyer.

Jade was nervous about spending so much time in the constant presence of a stranger; especially someone obviously as talkative as Rose. However, this trip was necessary to be ready for her new job. Jade was filled with a nervous excitement when she reviewed the events of the last five years. She realized her life was completely different than it had been then. Nick and Lisa had broken through her barriers gradually over the years, and if she were being honest, Nick had chipped away while Lisa smashed them all to bits. Her openness to those two amazing people still hadn't translated into a more global change of her life. She had still been grieving when she met them. But somehow, it was Joe's frightening reaction to her that caused her to wake up out of her virtual sleep. The scary incident with Joe had ironically forced a change she had previously been unable to initiate herself. In that light getting through, the forced companionship with Rose didn't seem as daunting as it should have. We made plans to meet on the following Sunday to drive to the Big Easy for the conference. That gave Jade the opportunity to unpack her boxes before she left for the conference. She couldn't help but breathe a sigh of relief being away from Joe; she hated feeling weak. Maybe he wasn't stalking her at all, but she felt better knowing he was too far away to be a threat.

Joe waited for Diana to get off of work. The good thing about his new job was that although he was sometimes on call, he had some flexibility. She had always been predictable, though. Diana arrived at work at 8:30am every day and left at 5:00 pm, but last week she went to a bar with a few friends from work. This morning she had gotten dropped off by some guy in an SUV. It sure hadn't taken her long to move on. Joe looked forward to talking to her real soon. He would make sure she was sorry she ever left him.

When You Least Expect It

Chapter 4:

On the Road to the Future

We can't know what's going to happen. We can just try to figure it out as we go along.
-Roger Sullivan

"Let me know if you need to stop." Rose said as they drove southward on the highway towards New Orleans.

"Will do."

"So this is your first year teaching?"

"Yes."

Rose paused, "I'm sorry. I'm not trying to be pushy. I guess I talk a lot. It's a terrible fault."

"No, I'm the one who should apologize. I guess I'm kind of quiet."

"That's no problem. I can do all the talking and you can do the listening."

"So, in answer to your question, yes, this is my first year teaching. What else do you want to know?"

"Well, you're from Chicago. Did you bring anyone with you from Chicago?"

"No, I didn't bring anyone with me. I'm single; no boyfriend, no husband. Is that what you were really asking?" Jade asked with a smirk.

Rose smiled, mischievously, "I promise that I'm done digging into your personal business."

"It's fine. Not much to dig into really."

"So…no boyfriend, huh?"

"Nope."

"Well there are a couple of teachers at school. I'm not sure exactly what their stories are, but Leo Blackbird and Mark Kane."

"Thanks, but no thanks. I have enough to worry about. I'm really not looking for, you know. I'm just here to teach."

"Hmmm…interesting, if you say so."

Jade just looked out of the side window.

"So, do you mind country music?"

"It's not my favorite but I don't mind it."

"How about some oldies?"

"That's fine, but really…"

"Oldies it is."

They drove for a little more than two hours, talking mainly about music before they stopped for a food break.

"How's this?" Rose asked, pulling into a burger chain restaurant.

Jade answered, "Perfect, I'm starved."

During lunch, they discussed what they would like to do after they arrived that evening.

"I think we need to go to Bourbon Street."

Jade coughed, trying to finish swallowing her drink. "Why do we need to go to Bourbon Street?"

"Well, you know what I mean. It's one of those New Orleans experiences."

"Yes, but I heard it gets pretty wild. I mean, that isn't really my kind of thing."

"Oh, you mean Mardi Gras? When they throw the beads at women?"

"Yeah, like that. I've always been too busy to do much partying. I'm not sure."

"Jade, I promise I'm not planning on taking my top off. Also, I promise if you get uncomfortable, we'll leave right away. There's probably a decent restaurant we can eat at."

"It's not that I'm afraid to go there, I'm just not a big drinker."

"Neither am I, but honestly…how often are you in New Orleans?"

Jade paused to consider Rose's words, "Okay. We'll go to Bourbon Street."

"Well first we'll finish lunch." Rose said, smiling.

"Great. Do you want some of my fries?" Rose offered.

"No, I'm good, but thanks."

They finished lunch and got back into Rose's car. "Are you sure you don't want me to drive for a bit?"

"It's fine. It's not a bad drive, but it probably would be if the weather was bad or I was by myself."

"If you're sure?"

"I am, but if you want to, go through the papers I printed out. We can figure out a plan of attack. When is our first workshop?"

"Eight in the morning I think. Or maybe that's just breakfast."

"Eight in the morning… Yikes, I haven't been up that early in over a month."

"Me neither. In fact, most of my classes were later in the morning."

"You get used to it."

Jade nodded and started looking at the information that Rose had printed out.

After a few minutes, she pointed out, "Hey, this ghost tour sounds kind of cool. I've never been on one."

"Do you like paranormal things?"

"Well, I had my tarot cards read once."

"Really? I always wanted to do that. What was it like?"

"Actually, I was surprised. The woman made a lot of sense. I guess it's one of those situations where you hear the right thing at the right time."

"Ooh, maybe I can get my cards read, but let's definitely look into the ghost tours. That is something I want to do for sure."

"Me, too. How much does it cost?"

"Well there are a few of them. I guess it depends on which specific one you choose."

"There are tours that are just ghosts and some that also have vampires and zombies. Weird."

"Yeah, well, I think there are coupons. We can look at them and see what the best deal is. Or maybe we should go online and see what the reviews say."

"That sounds like a great idea."

"Okay. I'll take a look through them and we can decide after we get to the hotel."

"Alright. Hey! Marie Laveau's Voodoo museum is on Bourbon Street. Wow!"

"You wanna go there?"

"I think so. I mean, I've heard of her. She was a Voodoo queen, right? I don't know anything about Voodoo."

"Me neither, but let's go there too."

"It might be interesting, but what about the swamp tour?"

"I don't think we have that much time."

"It's New Orleans. You have to take in the sites. It's imperative."

"I don't think its "imperative," but I guess it would be a waste of an opportunity."

"That's the spirit."

They chattered off and on for the next couple of hours of the drive about places Rose had been to. Jade hadn't traveled much beyond Chicago; just a trip to Disneyworld when her father was still around and a couple of weekend trips to Wisconsin with her mother and sister. When Rose parked the car, they checked into their shared room and headed for Bourbon Street.

"Wow," Jade exclaimed, looking around, amazed at the scene. Drunken revelers poured into the streets along with people wearing brightly colored costumes. There were scantily clad women in lingerie and stilettos advertising live shows from the doorways of buildings. "This is really—different."

Rose scanned her surroundings and agreed, "Yep. Do you suppose they have any good restaurants nearby?"

"I've heard that it's impossible to have a bad meal here. I guess we can either be brave and test the theory or be more scientific about it and check the guidebook."

"Well, we're here. Let's just find a place and take a chance."

"Sounds good to me."

They found a restaurant just off of Bourbon Street that wasn't too crowded and enjoyed a good meal. Afterwards, Jade located Marie Laveau's and they enjoyed looking at all the candles, fetishes, and other curiosities. The shop had a Tarot reader, but there were several people in line so Rose opted to come back before they left for home. Jade and Rose enjoyed the short walk back to their hotel and they went to bed early.

The next few days went by in a blur. They were busy during the days at workshops, but they took nights to just walk around in the French Quarter. In Jackson Square, they viewed the art on display from various local artists and found a restaurant nearby.

Jade suggested, "We should go back to Marie Laveau's. Maybe you can get a reading."

"It's worth a try."

"Oh, and afterwards, we can try one of those Hurricanes I heard about at lunch today."

"Sure."

Rose was able to get a reading. While she was in the back of the store talking to the spiritual adviser, Jade asked at the shop about ghost tours. The clerk pointed to a few flyers giving information on several.

"This place gives tours. In fact, I know who gives the 7:30 pm tour. He's really good. He knows all about the history of New Orleans."

"Sounds great. Thanks."

Rose emerged from the back of the shop and looked a little pale.

"So how'd it go?"

"Enlightening. Let's get that drink."

Jade was curious as to her reaction and wanted to ask more but realized that Rose would share more if and when she was ready. After all, they were colleagues who barely knew each other.

"Sure."

They walked a couple of streets until they found the bar that Jade had heard made the best Hurricanes and they walked through the crowded street, sipping on their drinks.

"So I heard about some ghost tours. They have one at 7:30 and 9:00 pm. I think I'd prefer to go to the earlier one, especially since we have morning sessions. Plus, the store clerk said her friend does the tour."

"Hmm, sounds good. We can do that tomorrow."

"Okay, let's plan on it. Ya know, I think I know why they call these Hurricanes It tastes great but I'm definitely starting to feel it. Wow."

"I know, right. Definitely don't want to have two of those."

"You want to head back to the hotel?"

"Why not? Not much else to do since we have things to do early tomorrow."

"I like New Orleans. I can't get over how friendly the people are."

"Me, too. It's definitely an interesting place, that's for sure."

"We have that session together right?"

"Yeah. So it's pretty intense, huh?"

"Yes, it is. I have to say that this reading program seems pretty intimidating. I hope I do it right. So much learn."

"You'll be fine. I'll be there if you have any questions."

"Thanks. I'm sure I will."

When they got back to the hotel, Rose turned on the TV and Jade got dressed in her pajamas and read a book for about an hour. After they turned off the lights, Rose spoke in the darkness.

"Do you believe in those tarot readings?"

Jade answered honestly, "Yeah, I do."

"Me, too. Goodnight."

"Night."

The next day they attended sessions all day and opted to eat a light dinner at the hotel before the ghost tour. On the way to meet the tour guide, they stopped into a couple of t-shirt shops to get a souvenir from the city.

The tour was good. The guide was knowledgeable about the seedier aspects of the city, but they weren't entirely convinced about the presence of ghosts and other paranormal beings. However, they returned to the hotel feeling a bit sad that the next day would be their last.

"It's funny that I feel pretty safe walking on the streets here. You always hear about the crime on the streets, but nothing's happened to make confirm it," Jade reflected.

"I feel pretty confident. I practice Karate."

"Really? I've always wanted to try that."

"You should. I practice 3-5 days a week at five in the evening. It gets a little bit tricky when school is in session. But, I get there."

"Are you a black belt?"

She laughed. "Not even close, I've only been doing it a year. I'm a green belt. I'm not exactly a ninja or anything, but I feel more confident. Plus, it's really relaxing."

"Relaxing?"

"Well, you can't think of anything else but doing the katas, punches, or kicks. Otherwise you screw up."

"That sounds really great. I would definitely be interested in trying it. I met this guy who got a little overly enthusiastic and well…I guess it would've been nice to feel a little bit more confident in taking care of myself."

"Oh my God, you had a stalker? That's scary."

"Well, not sure he was really a stalker but yeah, I was scared. It's like he couldn't take no for an answer, and he seemed to go from nice to pissed in seconds. He always showed up at work and the last straw was when he left a rose in my car, which was locked. I don't want to be one of those whiny females, scared of their own shadow. I want to defend myself if needed, ya know."

"Jade, you don't seem whiny to me, but I do know what you mean. No one wants to feel vulnerable."

They reached the hotel so Jade decided for a change of topic. "So tomorrow is the swamp tour, then we're on our way home."

"Yes, and I can't wait. I definitely want to come back here when I have more time."

"Me too."

"I guess we need to get packed for tomorrow then."

"Yeah, we have a long day ahead of us."

Rose and Jade were done with their conference at ten and then quickly headed to the swamp tour.

Jade fell in love with the swamp. She loved the airboat that zoomed through the marshes and waded through swamp grass. She marveled at the bald cypress trees with their knees jutting out of the water. She even laughed when Rose was startled when the tour guide surprised her by sticking a baby alligator in her face. Rose pulled away so abruptly that she nearly knocked Jade out of the shallow boat and into the swamp.

They talked all the way back to Nairobi. By the time they arrived back at the school parking lot, they had made plans to meet a few days before school to get their rooms ready and take the opportunity to go out for lunch.

"I guess I'll see you soon. You have my number if you need anything. Oh, Monday is karate. Are you really interested?"

"Yes, I'll call you later and get the information if that's ok…"

"Sounds great. Talk to you then."

They waved at each other as Rose drove out of the parking lot. Jade suddenly felt a little lonely at the thought of going back to her empty house. In a way it would be nice to have a nice quiet space again, but she thought about Rose's questions when they first started their drive. Rose had wondered about whether she had a boyfriend. Strangely, Jade realized that she hadn't spent any time thinking about being single before going to New Orleans. She had always been so busy working and going to school. It seemed like maybe it was time to open herself to the possibilities of being with someone. The future seemed ripe with opportunity. Jade was both scared and encouraged at the prospect of what the future might bring as she pulled up to the front door of her rental house.

Chapter 5:

Preparation

There are no secrets to success. It is the result of preparation, hard work, and learning from failure.
-Colin Powell

Of course, not everyone appeared on those few days before the start of school. She met the Principal and the Superintendent. She also met the secretaries, the other special education teacher, and the science and the math teachers. The teachers for physical education, art, and part-time family and consumer science, and computer instructors were not expected until the last day before student attendance.

However, the week prior to the start of school gave Jade the opportunity to scope out who to seek for help and who to avoid. On the eve before her first day, the most striking man Jade had ever laid eyes on appeared in the hall outside the classroom opposite hers. He was clearly Native American, around thirty years old with mocha skin. He had high, wide cheekbones and long, shoulder length black hair pulled into a ponytail at the nape of his neck. He was gorgeous. Jade couldn't be sure, but she thought he must be about five foot ten. His warmly colored skin was accentuated by his goldenrod colored Harley Davidson t-shirt. He was lean and muscular, like a swimmer. He was carrying boxes filled with art supplies, and Jade couldn't help but stare at his straining biceps and his firm rear end as he bent over to remove something from a box and disappeared into his classroom. The mystery hunk didn't look toward her classroom window where she was gawking at him, and it didn't occur to her until afterwards that she should have offered to help him, but no. That was definitely not a good idea. How could she talk to someone that gorgeous? It's not as though she was there in Nairobi to pick up guys, especially ones that she would be working with anyway. Jade obviously needed to get back to work.

About ten minutes later, the same stunning man swung the door to her classroom open without knocking and appeared briefly taken aback.

"I didn't know anyone was in here," he offered by way of explanation.

"Can I help you with something?" She said, slightly stunned by his abrupt appearance.

"My phone isn't working. I need to call the office and let them know."

"Go ahead. I'm Ja..." she stopped when he picked up the phone, appearing unconcerned with her for the moment.

After he talked to the office, he turned back at her, offering a tentative smile. "Sorry, I didn't mean to be rude. I'm the art teacher, Leo." He stood there expectantly, waiting for her to introduce herself. She seemed a bit confused for a brief moment, and then realized she had been staring at his smile, not really paying attention to what he had been saying. She felt her cheeks turn hot and color in embarrassment.

She quickly recovered and answered his question. "Sorry, I guess I'm a little bit nervous...big day tomorrow." She reached out to shake his hand. "I'm Jade Davis. I'm the new special education teacher."

"Your hands are ice cold. Leo took her pale hands into both of his much bigger ones. Absently, his tapered fingers gently rubbed her hands back and forth together between his callused palms. Her hands felt familiar to him somehow. It took a moment for him to realize that he had just met this woman and he was holding her hands.

Jade stared at his big hands and then looked up on the inside of his forearm at the brightly colored tattoo of two wolves. It was on the tip of her tongue to ask about them but he suddenly looked down and dropped her hands and slowly backed away. He turned to leave and said, "Gotta get back to it. I guess I'll see you around. Good luck tomorrow."

"Have a good night," Jade returned, feeling a little breathless as she realized she was talking to a closed door. Jade turned and stood in front of her desk, staring yet unseeing for a moment. She couldn't believe that after all this time and everything she'd been through, she finally met a man that made her want to look twice. She'd been through too much to get distracted by a handsome face. All the isolation of the last five years was finally getting to her. Jade definitely didn't need to screw up her new life by lusting after a fellow teacher. She needed to get a grip and do her best to keep things professional. Good thing she was going to have plenty to do in her first year just to stay on top of things. Jade took one last look at her desk and realized she was as prepared as she could be. Jade needed to be rested and ready for her first day.

"Shit, what did I do?" Was the first thought Leo had when he walked into his room? The uncomfortable answer was that he couldn't help himself. He had been getting along just fine these last few years in Illinois. He enjoyed teaching in Nairobi and he found a house with land that he loved. He even had a few friends. It was all good. Leo had adjusted to life alone, whatever the hell that meant! He had even gone on a few dates, but nobody had really blown him away until he walked into that classroom.

Jade really shocked him. She seemed to be unaware of her attractiveness, or maybe she was just a bit shy. Jade was really lovely and she was a special education teacher which meant that he couldn't really avoid interacting with her. It was going to be awkward looking at her everyday and trying not to make a fool out of himself.

"Jade," Leo thought to himself while he considered his ordered desk. He didn't know anything about her. She could be married or living with someone, so there was no sense in getting ahead of himself. The first couple of weeks would be really hectic anyway. He would do his best to get his infatuation under control, but in the meantime, he really itched to sketch her. "Jeez Leo—get a grip," he thought aloud, "Go for a workout. Tomorrow will be here soon enough."

Jade called Nick and Lisa when she got home that night. "So tomorrow is my first day."

Lisa was the main one talking but she was on speakerphone so Nick could hear too. "Honey, you're going to be great! You'll see."

"So what do you think of the other teachers? You must have met a couple by now. Any you'd consider as friend material?" Nick piped in.

"Yeah, don't start isolating yourself again." Lisa reminded her.

"Well…I've met a few people."

"So spill it. We want names, social security numbers…all relevant information."

"Jeez, Nick!"

"He's kidding, but we need some details."

"Well I met the other special ed teacher in the high school. He was a lot older and a bit weird. Then there's Rose from this summer and the art teacher."

"Art teacher? Male or female? Is he or she old or young? I need details here!"

"No, actually, Leo was pretty nice."

"Wait a second, Leo? Who is Leo? Spill!"

"Well he's the art teacher and there's nothing to spill. He wandered into my room because his phone wasn't working, so...he came into use mine. That's it."

"So this art teacher named Leo wandered into your room and he's what? Old? Troll like? I need adjectives?" You're being extremely vague here." Lisa demanded.

"Jeez, Lisa, take a breath! He looked Native American.."

"Ooh, nice."

"Lisa!"

"Okay, shutting up. Tell me more."

Nick jumped in, "Do you like him?"

"Let's not get ahead of ourselves, here. I just met him and we work together."

"Anyway, you were describing him before we interrupted you. Continue, please."

"Well he's taller than me, has long black hair, and smoky gray eyes."

"Ooh you really were paying attention, huh? Sounds good. Does he have a nice body?"

"Don't answer that, Jade. Leave her alone, Honey."

Jade changed the subject. "So how is the restaurant? Have you been busy?"

"Oh yeah. You know as long as the weather holds, but it won't be too long and we'll be knee deep in snow and wrapped up like mummies."

"That is something I won't miss. It doesn't get nearly as cold down here, although the rain is pretty unbelievable."

For a moment none of them spoke, and then Nick broke the silence, "Jade, we just want you to be happy and to make friends. We miss you. Don't start making excuses not to get close to people again, ok? Jade?"

She cleared her throat before responding, "I won't," Jade promised, adding, "I miss you guys, too."

"We'll see you at Thanksgiving. Call this weekend and tell us how it all went-or before if you want." Lisa says.

"Okay, I will."

"Text me and let me know how the first day went. Also, send me a picture of the hottie." Lisa finished in a whisper.

"I'll do my best." Jade said, just to get her off the phone.

She was still smiling when she went to bed. That night she dreamed about Leo the art teacher, who was indeed hot and off limits.

CHAPTER 6:

Teacher Institute

Remember tonight, for it is the beginning of always.
                                                -Dante Aligheri

"Desperado, why don't you come to your senses…"

Leo opened the door to the faculty lounge when he heard the most off key version of The Eagles "Desperado" ever sung. Jade was making photocopies on the faculty copy machine with ear buds in her ears, singing at the top of her lungs. She was obviously under the impression she was still the only teacher in the building. Leo was thoroughly charmed. He felt like applauding her performance, but he didn't want to embarrass her, so Leo just slipped into the bathroom and left before she noticed him.

He'd worked out last night after all, but he still found that he couldn't go to sleep until he sketched for a bit. He had ended up sketching an image of his hands combined with Jade's. It had felt so right in that moment. Leo's thirty year old self felt completely ridiculous to be so taken with this woman, but he also felt excited in a way he hadn't felt for a very long time.

The first day of school was a teacher institute, so all the teachers and staff in the district arrived a bit early and enjoyed a breakfast catered by the district. The high school library was buzzing with dozens of conversations, and people were gradually moving to tables to prepare for the inevitable beginning of the year speeches.

Rose was sitting at a table when she saw Jade and motioned her over.

"Are you still sore?" Rose whispered to Jade.

"Honestly? Yes, but just a little."

"Me, too. Did you enjoy it?"

"Oh yeah I can see what you mean about the relaxing part. Is the instructor always that intense?"

"His name is Shihan, and yes, pretty much. So you're going to keep going then?"

"Absolutely. I even stayed to watch the higher level class. I would love to be that good someday."

"Well they practice every day but if you stick with it—"

"Those katas look pretty hard."

"They're not easy but you'll learn. I can go through it with you sometime."

"Thanks. I would really appreciate that."

Cynthia, the junior high special education teacher, joined them at the table and Rose introduced them. Cynthia had a calm, unassuming presence that belied her constant chatter. She was five foot six with blonde hair and large brown eyes, in her thirties and a young Diane Keaton look alike. She wore shirts and sweaters that were so large they made her virtually disappear. She spoke very quickly, so it was almost impossible to hear all of what she was saying, and you really wanted to hear her because Cynthia (a thirty something young, Diane Keaton look-a-like) seemed to know the community really well—as well as the kids. Jack, the Information technology guy, walked by the table and Cynthia called out to him.

"Hey Jack. You need to set up the newbie's computer. This is Jade Davis, the new special education teacher."

"Hi." He said, offering a smile and a small wave. "I already did it this morning."

"Wow. You're good."

He chuckled, "I know. Well it's all about to begin so I better get a seat. See you guys later."

After about a half hour of announcements and speeches, Jade found herself looking around restlessly. Just then, Jade got tapped by Cynthia and Rose. Apparently the administration had announced the new hires and she was being asked to stand and introduce herself.

Jade suddenly felt overwhelmed. She had been accustomed to standing in front of groups of children and even a few adults at a time, but being on the spot in front of an entirely unfamiliar group of people filled her with a sudden panic. Jade momentarily contemplated bolting before her eyes fixed on a pair of intent gray eyes standing at the library entrance. Leo was there leaning against the doorway, staring at her intently. She concentrated on what he was wearing; a long sleeved white t-shirt that was rolled up to his elbows with and a pair of jeans and motorcycle boots. In that moment, she felt safe looking at him.

Suddenly she spoke as though speaking only to Leo. Their eyes remained locked until she was done telling the room full of high school employees where she was from, what school she attended and accepted her assorted welcomes from the surrounding employees. The moment her eyes lost contact with his and she glanced back at the doorway, he had disappeared. No one else seemed to notice the exchange though. It was almost as though she imagined him, but the fact that his presence seemed to comfort her was puzzling and slightly disturbing. She could do this. She had no room for a man in her life, especially right now. It was best.

'Well I'm in real trouble,' Leo thought to himself.

He wasn't sure why he just stayed there in the doorway, but when he saw Jade…well, she'd seemed panicked, so he just stayed right there. It felt in that moment like that was what she needed him to do, but why he believed that way made no sense. They didn't know each other, but it's like he knew what he needed to do for her. If his presence in the library doorway at that moment comforted her, he was glad. He was really starting to sound like his father. Ben had always talked about him needing to 'follow his inner voice.' Leo wasn't sure but he'd be damned if it didn't suddenly make sense to do just that though.

Four years. He had been teaching at Nairobi High School for four years and he had never been attracted to a fellow teacher. In truth, he hadn't been attracted to anyone since his wife passed away. He and Becca had known each other for what seemed like forever. When his world fell apart, Leo left. He needed to start again even though at the time he hadn't really held out much hope for a new beginning. There was something about Jade that called to him and for the first time in a long time, Leo felt nervous, but extremely optimistic.

Once all the new district hires were finished introducing themselves, more announcements were made, which would be followed up by meetings in our respective buildings for a more one-on-one basis. Jade looked back to the doorway Leo had just been standing in and tried to recapture the moment just as the head of the union, Edie, approached her. She offered her a "Welcome Aboard" and gave her an envelope full of forms that needed to be filled out as a new union employee.

When she headed out to her building, Jade caught sight of Jack, the I.T. guy. He was standing with a couple of other teachers and they all started talking at the same time.

"Don't let the kids intimidate you."

"They are a bit much, but you just have to get your bluff in early."

"Start off tough and later you can loosen up."

"Just call me if you need anything."

Jade got the names of the students on her caseload and had copies of each of her students' schedules printed out so she could give copies of their individualized education plans to each teacher so they would know what accommodations to follow. Jade worked through lunch to get it done. She felt bad about telling her new co-workers that she didn't have time to join them for lunch but she was starting to get nervous about her first day. *"I'm a real teacher,"* Jade thought to herself. She wondered if her mother would be proud.

Her mother, Jessie, was an art teacher at the high school and community college. She always wanted to spend more time on her art, being a gifted sculptor and photographer, but when her husband walked out on her and left her with two young girls to raise, she didn't have the opportunity to take the time off she needed. She had to be content to help her students become better artists at the local community college a couple nights a week after she got home from her high school teaching job. Jessie always seemed happy with her life but she had high hopes for her girls. She closed her eyes and said a silent prayer, "I hope I make you proud, Mom."

Eyes open again; she picked up her files and headed to the photocopy machine, ready to hand off copies of the students' records to the teachers. She was done copying in no time but it took a bit longer than expected tracking down teachers as they stopped in another teacher's room or went to the office to drop off paperwork, and so on. By the time she got to Leo's room, it was 3:30 pm and most of the other teachers had already left; making the most of the last hours before the new school year began. He was clearing off a metal shelf that would soon hold student projects before he looked up.

"I have some I.E.P's for you. I'm sure there'll be more, but these are the kids on your roster on my caseload so far." She said by way of explanation.

He looked at her for a moment before he smiled, taking the proffered documents. "Thank you."

Jade felt awkward, wanting to say more but not being able to think of anything. "Let me know if you need anything else." She said, turning back to the door.

"So you're from Chicago, huh? Does your family still live there?" Leo enquired quickly before she pulled open the door.

She turned back and hesitated for a moment, the light leaving her eyes as she frowned, "Not anymore. Where are you from? I can't place the accent."

"I'm from North Carolina."

She turned to look at his wall that was covered with drawings and art museum posters. "So what's your favorite medium?"

"I paint, mostly. Are you an artist?" He raised his eyebrows in question.

She shook her head and laughed. "No, actually I can't draw a stick man, but I love to look at art." She turned back towards the door, "You have the neatest desk I've ever seen." She said quickly, looking away from him.

"I like order." He replied, a little defensively.

"Seems a little strange for an artist to be so meticulous," She quickly added, "My mother was, well I mean, I thought artists were all sloppy?"

"I don't know. Maybe it's the teacher part of my personality that makes me more ordered." He replied smiling.

"Well I would be exceptional, then. I'm not neat and orderly." She said as she opened the door.

"I have no trouble believing you're exceptional."

Jade's face turned bright red and she responded. "Well I have some other I.E.P's to deliver so…" She left his classroom and slowly walked down the hall feeling a little stunned, not sure if he had been flirting with her or was just being nice.

He opened the door and called out to her, "You'll be okay. Just don't let them run over you."

Jade turned around and smiled, "I won't. Thanks."

His eyes twinkled, and he replied with an easy smile, "Goodnight, Jade."

Jade quickly returned to her classroom and after about an hour, walked out into the hallway. She noticed Rose and

Cynthia talking in the hallway on their way out. Cynthia certainly could talk. They noticed her and asked, "So did you ever eat any lunch?"

"I got so busy that I forgot."

Rose shook her head and replied, "Don't make a habit of that or you'll burn out too quick."

Cynthia then asked, "So are you all set?"

Jade looked down at her messenger bag crammed with books and papers, "I guess we'll find out tomorrow. I'm doing a lot of reviewing the rules, getting to know you, some written activities, and some that have them up and moving around."

"That sounds good! Don't forget to stay flexible. We have a lot of distractions around here like announcements being made just when you're starting out, people coming to the door, unscheduled assemblies. You'll get used to it eventually—or not." She laughed.

"My mom was a teacher and I volunteered in a classroom before so I think I know what to expect."

"Oh? What does she teach? Did she retire?"

"Actually, she died. It's been a few years now. She taught high school art and some college classes."

"I'm so sorry." They both said in unison. Rose asked the question she had been dreading.

"How did it happen?"

"Car accident-somebody had too much green beer I guess." She tried for a smile. "It was St. Patrick's Day and my baby sister was with her. It kind of ruined the holiday for me."

"That's horrible, Jade!"

"Really guys, I'm fine. It was a long time ago. It sucks but...Well anyway, I'll see you guys tomorrow. I'm going to get something to eat and head home. Maybe I should buy some groceries." How could I let that slip my mind?

Leo had just walked out of his classroom when he heard Jade mention that her mother and sister had died. He wondered if that was why she seemed so closed off. It was a familiar impulse. The other teachers at Nairobi were friendly, but they didn't push. It was a good place to hide at first when he was dealing with his own loss, and then one day after a few months, Leo realized that he didn't want to hide anymore. He wanted to find a new home and that meant he had to let some people in. He began talking to Jack. Leo learned one night that his wife had also died and he realized that even though it wasn't pleasant, common ground to share, but it was a means to begin to get to know Jack. Later he became more open to other people he worked with and at other places like the health club, his real estate agent after he bought his cabin, and a few of his neighbors.

Leo didn't really know what to make of Jade. She was a first year teacher. It wouldn't be easy for her being young and pretty. She might have some trouble being taken seriously, especially by the male students. Although, Leo remembered what his supervising teacher for his student teaching classes had warned them of, "No matter who you are and how unattractive you may perceive yourself as being, there is likely someone who you will come across in your teaching who may develop a crush on you." He had been teaching for seven years and thankfully hadn't had much of a problem with it, but it was important to be weary of students who were too clingy or flirtatious. Teenagers always tested your limits.

Leo felt drawn to her from the first time he saw her. Her eyes reminded him of jade, but there was something exotic, yet vulnerable about her. She was beautiful in a different way than Becca had been. She had fair porcelain skin and reddish blond hair where Becca had been a brunette with dark brown eyes.

Leo thought that he sensed a mutual attraction, even though Jade hadn't gone out of her way to talk to him. Everything about her screamed, "Proceed with Caution," as though she had some orange road cones placed around herself. He didn't really see the standoffishness as personal though. She didn't seem to get overly open or friendly with anyone. He figured that she was still dealing with grief on some level for her mother and sister. He certainly understood how hard it could be to try to come back from that kind of loss.

Leo had gone to the movies with friends and noticed all the couples. He missed that intimacy that he had once had with Becca, but he wasn't sure if you ever got that lucky twice in one lifetime. Leo walked out to his car. It was time to go home and relax and get ready for a brand new year. He thought of Jade and couldn't help but feel it might be an interesting one.

Joe sat in the parking lot in front of Jade's apartment building and watched someone else unload boxes to carry up to her former apartment.

"So Jade's gone, but that's ok. The great thing about the age of technology is it's all but impossible to disappear. Hell, she has to file a change of address. The post office is so nice about forwarding the new information once you send something to that address. I guess we'll be seeing each other soon, but in the meantime, Diana should be just about to leave work."

Catherine Scott

CHAPTER 7:

First Day of School

*And now we welcome the New Year, full of things
that have never been.*
 -Rainer Maria Rilke

Jade was the first teacher to arrive the next morning. She hadn't slept well. "Better to get there a little early and stay a little late," her mother always said. She decided to bring a box of donuts to put in the teachers' lounge. She wanted to be friendly and she realized that she was probably going to need a lot of help to get through the year.

The first day went pretty well. Jade mispronounced almost everyone's name. There were several absences and a few of the kids said that they missed Mrs. Franklin, who had been there last year, but that was to be expected. She was new. Change was hard, especially for kids.

All in all, her lessons went pretty well in the morning, but after lunch, students were a bit wild, talking about inappropriate things that had gone on over the summer. She had to send a couple of students to the dean of student's office to help them understand that she wasn't going to put up with their nonsense. One student let her know that she was wasting her time sending them to the office.

"I'm on the basketball team. Coach isn't going to do anything to me, lady."

Kayden, a tall, good-looking but angry young man that was apparently the star forward on the varsity basketball team, got in her face when she insisted that he stop talking. She answered back by standing on a chair in front of him so she would be even taller than him and told him, emphatically, to leave the room. He looked at Jade like she had lost her mind. It later occurred to her that the unorthodox move could have backfired on her. However, Kayden walked out without another word. After that the class became more manageable. The teenagers were still a bit talkative, but they did their work. At the end of the last period, Coach Bell stopped by for a visit. She told the students to keep it down so the few students who were still finishing assignments could finish while she went to find out what he needed.

Coach Bell got right to the point, "I saw Kayden. He can be a handful, but he's not a bad kid. I talked to him. I don't think you'll have any more problems out of him."

Jade let out the breath she had been holding in. She had been worried that the administration might not support her. "Well that's good to hear because he said that since he was on the basketball team, that you wouldn't do anything to him and I was wasting my time sending him out."

"Oh did he now? Well Mr. Long is going to be in for some laps. That's not how things operate around here."

"I didn't think so. I thought you would want to know what he said. I didn't think you were the type of Coach that thought it was okay to be disrespectful to his teachers."

"No, I certainly don't, and I want you to know that if you have any problems with any of the kids, just go ahead and send them to me. It'll take time to get them in check, but we'll do it."

"Thanks Coach, I will."

"You take care now, Honey. It's going to be a good year."

Jade rejoined the class and sat down at a table with a group of students who were playing Uno. She was just about to ask how the game was going when the bell rang. The students grabbed their backpacks and other belongings and scrambled out as fast as they could. Jade gathered up the games and started putting them away in the file cabinet when she heard someone knock on the door a minute before the classroom door opened. Leo stepped inside.

"So how did it go?" He asked tentatively.

She gave a small smile and answered, "Pretty well. I had to send one student out. He was one of the basketball players."

He raised his eyebrows and said, "That's always interesting. Who was it?"

She shook her head thinking that even though she was terrible with names, she was unlikely to ever forget his, "Kayden."

He shook his head. Leo was obviously familiar with Kayden, and said, "His sister is one of the aides here, Talia. Just talk to her about him and she'll help. Did you eat lunch?"

Jade hesitated a moment before answering, "I just ate a granola bar at my desk. I'm still trying to get a handle on things."

He looked at her with a hint of disapproval but only commented, "Well I'm just across the hall if you need back up."

"I appreciate that, thanks," she said in reply.

Just then, Jack stopped by to check her printer.

Jack came into Jade's room, quickly apologizing, "Sorry it took me so long to get here. I was stopped by three other teachers on my way." He then seemed to sense he had walked into the middle of a conversation and asked, "Is this a bad time? I can come back in the morning."

Leo just shrugged and turned to leave.

Jade quickly followed him to the door and tapped him on the shoulder. He turned and she said, "Thanks again, Leo. See you tomorrow."

"Sure."

When Jade walked back to her desk, Jack had already started examining her printer. He checked the cables and turned it off and on again. The printer didn't start on its own so he ran a test page and it still didn't print. He turned around to Jade who was reviewing her lesson plans.

"I'm not sure what's going on with your printer and I need to get out of here tonight. I'll stop by first thing in the morning." He explained.

"That's fine. If I have to I can print at home…" She replied, but quickly asked, "Jack, how long have you worked here?"

"Let's see, I think it's been ten years."

"I just wondered."

"Sure. So how do you like it so far?" He asked her. "This is your first year teaching, right?"

"It's great. I love the kids." She said as he grabbed her messenger bag and text books, following him out to his car.

"First year is rough. You always drive yourself crazy trying to be perfect, but it's an art, not a science. There are people here to talk to if it gets to be too much." He offered.

"Thanks, everyone's been wonderful so far." She confirmed.

"No problem. I better get home. My wife is already stressing about how late I am. See you tomorrow." He said apologetically.

"Well be careful, and goodnight," she said smiling.

In the parking lot she saw a motorcycle parked next to her Honda Civic and she wondered briefly about whom it belonged to. Leo had been wearing a Harley-Davidson t-shirt the first time she saw him, but that didn't necessarily mean anything.

One thing was certain. Leo had certainly peaked her interest.

On the way home, Jade stopped at Lucky's convenience store in town about five minutes from her house. It was the only contact she had outside of Nairobi, and she liked the women who worked there. They seemed friendly to the customers without being nosey. Maddie, the assistant manager, always seemed to be working when Jade stopped by on her way home. She was about the same age as Jade but she was a couple of inches shorter with an olive complexion and long, dark brown hair that she usually wore in a braid. Maddie was a flirt. She always seemed to get a lot of attention from the male customers.

"Hey, you sure do like diet coke." You know it would probably be cheaper for you to just go ahead and buy a case at Wal-Mart."

"Probably, but I like fountain soda." Jade replied.

"Works for me. Where are you from anyway?"

"Chicago."

"What are you doing down here?"

"I teach over at Nairobi."

"Wow, I hear it's pretty rough over there."

"Not really. My students are great. The town is a little run down, but there are a lot of good things happening there now."

"Well that's good. I wish you taught here. My son Chris is having a hard time with his math teacher. I swear he's only in the 5th grade and I already have no idea how to help him with the work his math teacher is giving him. You wouldn't have time to tutor him, would you?"

"Sure, why not."

"I couldn't pay much, but I could make you dinner."

"Sounds good. Maybe this weekend?"

"I'll make sure Chris brings his book home. He likes to try to tell me he doesn't have any homework but Mr. Matthews says he always has some practice work to do."

"Here's my number. Just give me a call." She wasn't going to turn down a dinner, especially if she didn't have to make it.

Nick had been doing paperwork in the restaurant after the lunch rush when he noticed an email from Al.

"Sorry to hear about Joe and your friend. I'm not sure what's happening with him. My mother mentioned something about him being in a car accident and trouble with a girlfriend, but I don't know any details. I'll contact my mom and see if I can find out anything else. I'll let you know."

Nick answered the email, "Thanks, Al. Keep yourself safe. A care package is on the way."

Nick wasn't sure what to think about Al's email. He didn't know if there was any point in calling Jade about it. None of it really raised any red flags, but Nick would discuss it with Lisa when she got home from her doctor's appointment. He hoped she was feeling better.

    Jade knew that everyone was right about taking time to get out of the classroom to take a break for lunch, but she couldn't make herself do it. Being a teacher was a lot more complicated than she had realized. In school she was taught that the goal was to teach content to students at their individual levels and to have an understanding of various disabilities as well as assisting other teachers in making instructional accommodations and modifications, but there was so much more to do.

    There was the refereeing of fights between students, the calls home to parents, intervening personality clashes between regular content area instructors and administrators, as well as the daily hassles of students who showed up regularly without needed basic materials. Jade just didn't feel like she was ever going to be on top of things. She was always anticipating—seldom able to relax and enjoy her students. The thing was she really liked the kids and she felt they were gradually starting to trust her. Rationally, she knew that she couldn't continue to keep up at this pace, but after four weeks of being the first teacher to come in and the last to leave, Jade was exhausted.

Leo had finally decided to take a more direct approach. He showed up at her classroom door just after the lunch bell rang and forced the issue.

"That's it, you cannot keep doing this." He insisted with his arms folded over his chest and a grim expression on his face. "Let's go to lunch."

Jade started to protest, but realized she was being foolish to resist taking the time out. She needed to take a break so she would be fresher in the afternoon. Jade also realized that spending time with other teachers was important for political survival in a school building.

A few teachers looked with interest when Jade walked in ahead of Leo. He offered her a chair, and she sat down. Then Leo walked back out of the lounge without saying anything. Jade felt a bit awkward sitting in the small room, watching her co-workers eat but she didn't get much of a chance to reflect on that because she was immediately bombarded by questions.

"So you're from the Chicago area, right?" Rich Stanley, the other high school special education teacher asked.

"Yes." She confirmed, "I was raised in the suburbs, actually. Where are you from?"

That was the last thing she was able to say because another teacher walked in immediately complaining about a student's behavior in the hallway. Jade tried to follow the conversation but she really only caught bits and pieces. She wasn't familiar with many of the students' names, so she had a hard time following the discussion. She stood to go to the vending machine and bought a diet soda, but before she sat back down, Leo had reappeared in the doorway carrying two trays of food. He put one down in front of her and then sat next to her to begin to eat from his own. The food looked like the typical cafeteria offering; chicken patty on a bun, apple, carrot sticks and ranch dressing. "I could have gotten my own food."

Leo just smiled.

She mouthed, "Thanks." As Jade began to eat her own food, she realized that she was hungrier than she realized. As everyone began to dispose of their trays and left over wrappers on their way out, Jade turned to Leo, "So I guess it's time to go back."

He nodded in confirmation and emptied the garbage from both of their trays and followed her out into the hallway. Turning back to her he inquired, "See, the world is still spinning, even though you took a twenty-five minute break. It wasn't so bad, was it?"

Jade offered a big smile, "No, it really wasn't. I promise I'll start making time for myself so thank you, Leo. I appreciate you taking the time to consider me."

He smiled back, "Come on…we better get back to our classrooms before the bell rings or the kids will run us over." She laughed and they walked back to their rooms, but didn't quite get to them before the students arrived.

Jade felt much more relaxed after having lunch in the teachers' lounge. She was grateful to Leo for pushing her to take that time out and she realized that she not only was attracted to him physically, but she genuinely liked him. He was warm and funny. Jade still felt that she didn't need to get attached to Leo, but she couldn't bring herself to care.

She continued to go to lunch with Leo. He would appear at her door or she would go to his, but they always went together, but that only lasted until the first Friday in December.

Joe hadn't talked to or seen Nick since the incident at the restaurant, but he knew that bitch Jade had moved away. Thanks to the internet though, it wasn't hard to trace her. Moving a few hours away wouldn't keep Joe from paying her a visit. A long drive sounded like a really good idea. Diana hadn't enjoyed their 'reunion.' He had seen her laughing and talking with some guy coming out of a bar and he snapped. Luckily, he had been driving a truck from work. They hadn't been smiling once he had plowed right into them. Joe knew that any witnesses to the scene would assume it had been a random hit and run, probably by a drunk driver. He didn't know how badly his ex or her new boyfriend was hurt, and he didn't care. Diana wouldn't be smiling again anytime soon, and that made him smile.

Jade knew there were no scheduled meetings but she'd been called at the last minute, twice the week before, and that she wasn't prepared for. She knew that paperwork was part of being a teacher, but it was definitely not her favorite part.

The phone rang in her room just after the last bell rang. It was the main school secretary, Aleesha, "There's someone here to see you."

As Jade walked out of her classroom towards the office, she noticed that Leo was still in his room. She really didn't need to get attached. Jade was thinking about Leo all the way to the office. She'd hoped it wasn't obvious to anyone, especially Leo, how attracted she was to him. It really wasn't fair that someone so good looking was so nice, yet so inaccessible.

When she reached the office, all thoughts of Leo evaporated when she saw who waited for her. A tall, middle aged man with the same dark green eyes as her own appeared in front of her. It had been more than 10 years, but she would have known him anywhere.

"Jade, you look so beautiful. Just like your mother." Her father said.

"Don't you dare talk about my mother," She seethed, "Not ever. I want you to leave right now."

"Can we go somewhere?" Her father asked quietly.

Jade didn't answer him and she didn't want to cause a scene, so she opened the office door and walked out and headed left toward the front door. Luckily there was no one around outside. She definitely didn't want to have a confrontation with her estranged father in front of students or their parents, either.

He followed her outside into the cool, cloudy afternoon.

"What do you want?"

"I wanted to see you. I know I should have come sooner…"

"You think?" She said with venom in her voice. "When do you think you should've come? Maybe when my sister was born? How about when we lost the house because Mom couldn't afford to pay the mortgage? Or how about when I buried Mom and Sarah alone? When is it that you think you should have come?"

"I don't know what to say," He sighed, "I can't change what's happened—"

Jade cut him off quickly, "No you can't and you're way too late. I've been fine without you and I prefer it that way."

"I know you're angry and I can't blame you. I've made a lot of mistakes, but you don't know the whole story. Things happened that you know nothing about. I'm so—"

"Just shut up. You didn't have time for me then and I don't have time for you now. I'm going to go back to thinking that you're dead. Don't come back. There's no one left that wants anything to do with you."

He tried to reach for her shoulder and Jade backed away and put her arms up.

"Just get away from me. You can't be here!"

He started to walk towards her again and she put her arms up to warn him off. "I don't know how you found me and I don't care, but want you to go back to wherever it is you came from, and stay there."

He started to walk towards her again, but acknowledged her grim expression, and thought better of it.

She then walked quickly back into the office and tried to compose herself.

"Aleesha, if that man ever comes back here, call the police."

She looked back at her, the shock clear in her expression, "Are you ok?"

"No, but I will be. Thanks Aleesha...Have a good night."

"You too."

She looked like she wanted to say more but didn't pry.

Jade barely felt the door close at her back before fat tears began to stream from her eyes.

She saw Jack come out of a classroom and walk quickly towards her.

"You okay?" He asked putting his hand on her shoulder.

She started to cry in earnest and spit out. "No."

"You want to talk about it?" He replied searching her expression.

She turned and walked into the teachers' lounge and Jack followed slowly behind her. Jade headed straight for the vending machine and put change in to buy a diet soda. Then she sat in a chair at the table and stared at her hands in front of her. He sat in a chair across from her and waited for her to speak.

She finally took a breath and spat out, "Fifteen years ago, my father went to work like every other morning and he never came back. My mother was pregnant with my little sister at the time. Anyway, I always assumed he was dead.

Why else would he leave and never come back?" She stopped to take a breath. "Well, he came to the school. Just now, like nothing ever happened." She swiped at the furious tears that relentlessly streaked across her cheeks stained pink from anger.

Leo had walked into the lounge just as Jade started to speak and raised his eyebrows to Jack in question. He had already been incredibly attracted to Jade and her distress called out to him, whereas Jack was clearly torn between empathy and a natural male aversion to tears.

"I hate crying, especially about him. He's not worth it." Jade continued, "I told him I don't need him and he should just go away and not come back. That bastard disappeared for fifteen years. He let me bury my mother and sister by myself. So many things happened and I was alone. He ...."

Leo crossed the room and stood behind Jade. He held her shoulders while she cried. Jack spoke softly.

"I don't know. Maybe at some point you'll be able to talk to him and find out his side of things," he suggested. She looked up at him with a dubious expression and he quickly put his hands up in surrender. "Not now, but at some point you may be ready to ask him for some answers, for your own sake." After a moment, he looked at his watch, "Guys, I need to get out of here. Things always look better after a good night's sleep. Maybe you could go have a beer and relax a bit," he concluded, nodding at Leo.

"I'm gonna go home now. Text me later and let me know that you're okay. G'night, kiddo." He said as he backed out of the room, looking as if he wished he could say more.

She shook her head, still too upset to speak.

Leo just sat for a moment and let her breathing return to normal.

"Let's get out of here." Leo said hopefully.

She didn't move for several minutes, and so he repeated, "C'mon, you need something to eat." Leo said more insistently as he pulled her chair out.

"I don't feel like eating anything." She replied.

"Well too bad, let's go. We'll stop by your room and get your things."

"Why don't you just go?" she said weakly.

Leo shook his head and frowned, "Sorry, afraid you're stuck with me for tonight. Go splash some water on your face and we'll get a pizza. I'll get your bag and your coat and meet you by the back door."

She looked at him for a moment seeing, the resolve in his face and finally said, "Okay. I'll only be a few minutes."

Five minutes later he met her at the back door and helped her put her coat on, then carried both his and her messenger bags.

They walked silently to her car and he grabbed her keys to put her bag in her trunk. They walked across to his truck and he opened the passenger door for Jade. Once Leo sat himself in the driver's seat, he picked up his cell phone and ordered a large pizza for pick up, then drove out of the school parking lot. Fifteen minutes later they picked it up and he headed to his house. Leo grabbed the pizza from the backseat of his truck and came around the side door. Jade looked through the passenger window as Leo opened the door.

"This is your place?" She asked quietly.

"We'll watch a couple of stupid movies and eat some pizza." He answered.

Jade raised her eyebrows but got out of the truck and followed him through the back door of the house, past the kitchen and into the living room where he sat the pizza down onto the coffee table.

"What do you want to drink? I have beer, diet soda, juice and water."

"Just water, please."

"Have a seat, or better yet, pick out a movie. The DVD's are on the back wall."

She just stood there in front of the back wall that was filled with dozens of movies and stared unseeing. Leo looked at her still stunned face and reached to an anthology of Abbott and Costello movies.

"It's impossible to be upset when you watch Abbott and Costello."

She sat down and he handed her a paper plate with a piece of cheese pizza and put a tall glass of ice water in front of her. He took the movie out of the case and looked back at her, "Ever seen Abbott and Costello Meets Frankenstein?"

She smiled a little sadly, "I remember seeing that when I was a kid. We watched channel 9 in Chicago that showed old horror movies called Creature Features. My mother, sister and I watched it nearly every Saturday night. I remember Abbott and Costello Meets Frankenstein was one of them."

"I'm sorry. We could watch something else. I have a lot of movies…"

"It's ok, Leo. It's a good memory. Let's watch the movie."

The movie started and Leo sat down on the couch about a foot away from Jade, but his eyes moved back and forth between her face and the TV screen. She finished her pizza and slowly seemed to relax. After the first fifteen minutes had passed, she started to laugh a little bit; self-consciously at first, but her face slowly spread into a smile. He scooted closer to her and pulled her head into his shoulder, rubbing the side of her face. Gradually her eyes began to flutter closed and Jade fell asleep right there, curled up next to him. After a few minutes, Leo slowly gathered her up and carried her to his bedroom and placed her on the bed. He covered her with his blanket and took a minute to kiss her on the forehead before he walked back out to the living room.

Jade awakened suddenly. She was puzzled, not sure where she was until she remembered Leo bringing her over to his house and falling asleep on his couch, curled up next to him. She made her way to the living room to find Leo lying on the couch with a small blanket partially covering his lower torso. He was wearing only a pair of pajama pants, leaving his lean, muscular chest exposed. Leo had dropped everything to help her feel better. She had to admit, something felt so right being with him. Maybe it was time to consider letting someone in.

Leo had a hard time sleeping on the living room sofa. He was worried about Jade and he was also distracted by the knowledge that Jade was in his bed. Leo startled when he felt a touch his shoulder. When he looked up, it was Jade, staring down at him.

"Why are you sleeping out here?"

"Because you were in my bed."

She grabbed the blanket off of him and reached for his hand.

Leo said warily, "Jade?"

"You can't sleep out here and I don't want to be alone." She explained.

"Are you sure?" He asked again.

"Just come lay down next to me." She said, squeezing his hand.

He nodded and followed her into the bedroom. She lay back down on the bed and pulled his hand to encourage him to join her. He gently kissed her forehead and pulled her across his broad chest and they fell back to sleep that way; each comforted by each other's presence.

CHAPTER 8:

Getting Close

Scared and sacred are spelled with the same letters. Awful proceeds from the same root word as awesome. Terrify and terrific. Every negative experience holds the seed of transformation.
-Alan Cohen

Jade didn't call Lisa until the next afternoon. Lisa was frantic by the time she called. "Oh my God, Jade…"

Jade immediately went on alert. "Lisa, what's wrong?"

"I went to the doctor. I can't believe it."

"What is going on, Lisa? I'm freaking out! Whatever it is, I'm here, well, I know I'm not really literally there, but talk to me."

"I'm pregnant!"

"That is the most amazing news ever! I bet Nick is over the moon. I'm so excited for you guys! I told you it would happen."

"I can't do this. I know I wanted to be a mother and Nick will be so great, but..." Her words ended in strangled sobs.

"Honey, please calm down. Just take a deep breath. He's going to be so happy."

"I know, but what if I suck at it. What do I know about being a mother?"

"You're the most nurturing person I know. You're going to be so great. Come on, Honey...Relax."

"Okay, I'm breathing. I'm still not sure."

"Well you are going to be awesome. I'm going to be a godmother. You and I are going to go shopping and find all kinds of adorable baby clothes. I'll take a day off and come up, and we'll go out to eat, shop, eat ice cream and pickles, or whatever it is you'll be craving."

"Ooh, don't say that. It sounds disgusting! I don't have any cravings. I'm just a little emotional and nauseous."

"Yuck. Have you been throwing up?"

"No, more like seasick."

"Well that's good."

"Yeah, I feel okay. Just nervous I guess. I need to tell Nick, but I'm a little scared."

"Honey, this is all just hormones. You're going to be an amazing mother, I swear! Now where is he?"

"He's in the restaurant wondering what the hell is wrong with me. I've been snapping at him all day."

"First thing you do is go find him and put him out of his misery. I'm going to stay on the phone. Just put the phone down and bring him in the office. I'll be on the line for moral support."

"Okay."

A minute or two later, Jade heard the door close to the office and the sound of footsteps. Leo walked into her classroom and Jade raised her finger to her lips, indicating the need for quiet. He sat in Jade's chair and silently waited, watching her curiously.

She then heard Lisa speak to Nick. "Jade is on the phone. I'm putting the phone on speaker because I need her with me while I say this."

"Okay, I'm really worried now. What's wrong, Honey? You look pale."

"Well I went to the doctor and I got some test done. I got the results."

Jade could hear the concern over the phone. "Whatever it is, Lisa, we can get through it together."

Jade jumped in. "Lisa put the man out of his misery!"

"I'm going to have a baby? We're pregnant!"

"A baby! You're having a baby? Why were you scared to tell me?"

"Because I'm afraid I won't be a good mother? I know that's what we wanted, I mean all of those forms…we filled out for adoption and they didn't like that we both work and everything, but—"

"But you could work from home. We can do anything together, you know that!"

Lisa was crying now but also laughing. She could hear the sounds of kissing over the phone and after their smooch fest, Nick spoke to Jade. "It looks like I have some reassuring to do. I think we'll be closing the restaurant early."

"That sounds like a plan. I love you guys. Call me tomorrow."

"We love you, too."

Leo walked over to Jade and when she saw he had tissues, she realized she was crying.

"You okay?"

"Yeah. It's really great news. My best friends are having a baby."

"That's great. So it was unexpected?"

"That's an understatement. They've been trying for years. They had all the tests. Lisa went through all the treatments, but nothing worked, so they had given up. They were trying to adopt, but it was taking forever."

"That's life. Sometimes great things happen when you least expect them to." His gaze was intent when he said it and for a moment, Jade could swear his eyes glanced at her mouth before he cleared his throat. "It looks like a celebration is in order, then. Chinese or Mexican?"

"I should be making some copies. Plus I have two IEP meetings on Friday that I need to get ready for."

"Tell you what. I'll make your copies for you and you can concentrate on the meeting stuff. Give me what you need copied."

"Alright, if you're sure?" She said handing him papers. "I already have a post it on there that says how many of each I need."

"I'm sure, and I'm hungry so hurry up and finish." Leo said as he walked out of her classroom.

Thirty minutes later he came back in with stacks of copies.

Jade smiled up at him. "Thanks. Well I'm not completely done, but I can get the rest done tomorrow."

"Right, let's go. You can follow me to Cape or I can drive?"

"I'll ride with you."

Jade considered him as they walked out to his truck. He was really good looking, but he was also the nicest person she had ever met. He made it so easy to be with him, like a calm she had never felt with a man. As strange as it was to admit, Jade was twenty-six years old, but she had never really been in a relationship.

She and Leo hadn't discussed spending the night at his house the night before, but that's what happened. They'd made no big deal about any of it, just got up in the morning and dressed so Leo could take her to her apartment to change her clothes. They then drove to work as though it was something they did every day. Nothing about it felt wrong or even awkward, except for the butterflies in Jade's belly.

She recalled he had been so beautiful lying on his back in sleep with his high cheekbones and long, black hair loosely flowing over his shoulders. He had smelled so amazing when she stirred, gently pulling herself away from his lean muscular chest. It was a clean citrusy smell that probably had something to do with cleaning his paint brushes. She had loved waking up stretched across his chest. Jade had itched to run her hands over the planes of his abs, but she hadn't touched him. Jade had gone into the bathroom and gotten dressed. When she came back into the room, he had already started gathering clothes for the day, and neither of them spoke about it, letting the moment pass. It's not as though she really knew what to do when it came to sex.

She had almost done the deed with a friend after prom just so they could both "get it over with," but she realized there were worse things than being the last virgin in high school. Now, it was really hard to admit that she was in her mid-twenties with no *real* sexual experience, because making out didn't count.

Not that she set out to "save herself," but her life had been about working towards a set of goals. Dating and sex was a distraction that she never really took the time to consider. For the first time in too long, Jade had the opportunity to start getting close to someone, but she didn't really know how. She didn't know how to even start up a romantic relationship, especially when she barely knew how to be a friend.

Leo drove the 30 miles to Cape Girardeau through winding roads westward into the waning sunset. He hadn't been able to concentrate on anything all day by being alternately aroused and mooning. His distraction had been obvious to his students, but he was able to pass it off as a lack of sleep. It was true that, Leo hadn't gotten a lot of sleep. At first, he had slept poorly for a couple of hours on the couch, trying not to think about her being in his bed. Then she asked him to stay with her. Once he joined her, he stroked her back through his shirt that he had just given her and toyed with her hair as she slept. Leo had wanted to kiss her. Actually, he more than wanted to kiss her. He was getting weary of being just friends with her but he didn't want to rush her. Leo knew that she was worth waiting for.

Pulling himself back into the present, he smiled at her sitting next to him in the truck cab, lost in her own thoughts. She looked beautiful staring out the window in the waning sunlight. Finally, he pulled into the driveway of a Mexican restaurant.

"We haven't been here before, but you like Mexican food, right? The food is here is good. If nothing else, they have steak and chicken so I'm sure you'll find something you like."

"I like Mexican food, especially the chips." Jade said with a big smile.

He held the door open for her and they walked into the crowded restaurant. Jade was glad that they were seated immediately and given a basket of tortilla chips and salsa. She tried not to eat too many of them before her food arrived. She ordered a beer and the Pollo Loco, while Leo ordered a

Chile Relleno plate. While they waited, Jade asked Leo about teaching on the reservation.

"In some ways it's very similar to Nairobi. Everyone there knows everyone else. Most of the staff feels like they have the right to boss each other around like a family member, even if they're not. Of course, I grew up there, too. So in answer to your question, it's great, but sometimes you have to move on." He finished with a sad smile.

"So you just needed a change of scenery?" She paused, and then continued, "Sorry. I'm not trying to pry."

He took a breath before answering. "Actually, no, my wife died and it was…well, it was too hard to be there anymore."

For a moment, Jade thought about asking for details, but she figured that he would tell her when he was ready. "I'm so sorry. I can understand, just in a different way. My mom and sister were killed by a drunk driver. After that, well, I kind of walked away from everything. I moved and went to school and got my teaching degree, but to lose your wife? I don't know what to say."

"Loss is loss. Anyway," he reached across to squeeze her hand, briefly, "we're a fine pair, aren't we?" He raised his beer for a toast, "To making happy memories from now on, and to your friends and their baby."

"To Nick and Lisa."

She picked her beer up and tapped it against his, and then they both took a swig. He smiled at her and she couldn't help but smile back. Their eyes remained locked for a moment. Something like longing passed briefly between them, but the spell was broken when the waitress brought the food.

She left the steaming plates in front of them, offering an apologetic smile, "I'm so sorry the food took so long. The kitchen is really slow tonight because we're short staffed."

Leo smiled at Jade as he put his napkin is his lap and replied, "I didn't notice."

They didn't say anything for several minutes while they ate their food. He tried to give her a bite of his Chili Relleno and she shook her head. "Not much for spicy stuff, but thanks."

He said with a mischievous grin, "Aww, come on. Just try a little bite."

"Well, maybe just a little bite, but I don't think I trust you." Jade said in answer. She felt like they were flirting.

She started to reach across with her fork, "Here, open up." His eyes gleamed with amusement.

"Alright, but if this burns my tongue…" she said in warning. She bit into it and her eyes went wide. He quickly handed her his beer to put out the fire as he chuckled. "I am so going to pay you back for that, Blackbird!"

He smiled back at her with a flirtatious grin, "Oh, I look forward to it, Ms. Davis."

After a few moments, Leo broke the silence. "So how do you know Nick and Lisa? Are they family friends?"

"No, they're my family. Actually, when I was in school, I worked for them as a waitress."

"Really? You waited tables? I've never done that."

"It's good in some ways, at least at their restaurant. They have a lot of regulars and I did some waitressing in high school, too."

"So you were saying about your friends?"

"Well, I started working for them after I started college. I was pretty closed off, still dealing with my family being gone, but Lisa wasn't having it. She's impossible to ignore. You'd have to meet her to understand."

They finished up their dinner and walked out to the parking lot closely, side by side. Their hands sometimes bumped into each other's. As always, Leo opened the truck door for her and waited for her to sit down so he could close the door behind her. But instead of just getting into sit down, Jade leaned into him, kissed his cheek and gave him a quick half hug before sliding into the bench seat. Leo closed the truck door and came around the vehicle to get into the drivers' side. Neither of them said anything on the drive to Jade's car. Leo was tempted to suggest that she just stay at his house, but wasn't sure how that would sound. Still, he really didn't want the evening to end as he pulled up beside Jade's car.

Before he could say anything to that effect, Jade spoke, "I'm not really tired yet, are you?"

"You wanna pick up some ice cream? We could try another movie night?"

"Sounds good. Follow me—we'll stop and pick up some ice cream on the way." Jade agreed and laughed as she got into her car.

As she watched the lights of Leo's pick up ahead of her, she realized that there was an increasing attraction between them; at least on her part. She wasn't sure about how Leo felt. Sometimes she was sure it was mutual, but other times she let her insecurities take over, causing her to feel as if she wasn't his type. She wasn't anxious to tip the scales either way because at least for now, it was perfect. She really loved spending time with him. He was so comfortable to be with. She had no desire to push the issue for the sake of clarity; no matter how good she felt when she was with him or how much space he took up in her thoughts when he wasn't. It wasn't worth the risk to push things in hopes of something more.

As planned, they stopped at a small store just before they closed. They bought a pint of moose tracks and shared it out of the container as they watched an 80's movie marathon on cable. They sat on the couch, pressed up against one another and laughed and talked about nothing serious until they fell asleep, curled up on his couch. At 5:00 am, Jade's cell phone alarm went off and she woke up in a fog. She realized that she had been asleep on the couch with him, curled protectively around her. It suddenly felt terrifyingly intimate, even though they were both fully clothed. Jade unwrapped herself from Leo's comforting embrace and escaped to the bathroom.

"Shit. What am I going to do?" She just stood there, feeling terrified as she leaned against the sink until Leo knocked on the door.

"Everything ok in there?" He asked.

Jade opened the door and there was Leo leaning on the door frame with a concerned expression. "I'm sorry. I guess I'm not really awake yet." She explained as she tried to breeze by him, but he grabbed her wrist to stop her.

"Are you sure you're good? You look upset."

"No, of course not, I'm just thinking about everything I have to get done." She replied with a schooled expression.

Leo raised his eyebrows in disbelief.

"Seriously, I'm going to go home and get ready for work. I'll see you later."

He stared at her for a minute and finally said, "Okay."

While she walked to her car she thought to herself, "I'll just have to take a step back. I'm obviously starting to spend too much time with him. Changing that isn't a problem. It's just a crush and I'll get over it. It'll be fine." Except it didn't feel fine; the thought of staying away from Leo made her feel sick.

Jade took the train up to Chicago the next morning where Lisa was waiting for her. "Oh my God, I can't believe how good it is to see you."

"Me, too. Let me see the little baby bump."

Lisa laughed, "I have too many clothes on it. I'll show you when we get home." They hurried to Lisa's car which was parked on the street.

"It's freezing here. I can't believe the difference a few hundred miles makes. I definitely don't miss the cold."

"Don't worry. The house is plenty warm. So what's going on with you? We were worried you might not come home for Christmas."

"Why wouldn't I?"

"Come on. He's taller than you, hot, you work with him... ringing any bells?"

"His name is Leo, and we're just friends," Jade told her softly and turned away, looking out the window.

"Oh, Honey."

Jade changed the subject. "Anyway, I can't wait to see what you have for the baby. We have to go shopping."

"Nick's already painted the baby's room blue and green. He says he'll paint over it if we find out we're having a girl," she laughed. "We'll find out in three weeks."

"You said he's been really overprotective lately?"

"Yeah, he's driving me crazy—always bugging me to sit down and rest. He won't let me do anything."

"But, the doctor says you're healthy, right?"

"Yes, the baby is fine and so am I. Everything is great, so don't you start too."

"I can't promise anything, but it's so great to see you. Are we going by the restaurant?"

"Not tonight. He's closing up early so we can all go out to celebrate your homecoming."

"We really don't have to. We can just order a pizza or something."

"We want to, and don't ruin this for us."

"I'm sorry. I'll shut up." Just as Lisa parked the car, the door opened at the same time her cell phone indicated a text message.

Nick pulled Jade out of the car and wrapped her up in a fierce hug. "Can't breathe!"

"Sorry, Sweetie. Where's your boyfriend?"

Jade stared at him and then at Lisa before she replied, quietly. "He's not my boyfriend. He's a friend and we work together, but that's it." She looked down at her phone and noticed the text message she received was from Leo. "Excuse me guys, I have to go to the bathroom." They shared a look but didn't respond.

When Jade closed the door to the bathroom, she read Leo's message.

Leo: "Hey, I just wanted to make sure you got to the frozen north okay. Text when you can. ☐

Jade: I'm here. They asked me where you were. I guess I talk about you more than I thought. Leave it to them to pay attention.

The phone rang immediately. Just as Jade answered, she hears, "You talk about me?"

"Maybe once or twice. Where are you?"

"Waiting for my flight to leave."

"Mmm, I guess we're going to go out for dinner."

"Well I hope you have a good time. Say hi to Nick and Lisa for me."

"Thanks. What time will you get to your Dad's?"

"It'll be late."

"Text me and let me know you made it."

"Will do."

"Night, Leo."

"Goodnight, beautiful."

When Jade opened the door to the bathroom, Nick and Lisa were standing there waiting with smiles on their faces. "Ready for dinner?"

"Sure am. Let's go."

Jade enjoyed her time with Nick and Lisa. Lisa and Jade shopped for baby clothes and took a day to pamper themselves as part of Nick's Christmas gift to them. She hung out with them at the restaurant for several days and enjoyed catching up with the regulars. But as much as she enjoyed visiting Nick and Lisa, she missed Leo. Something had to change. She couldn't ignore her feeling for him anymore, so when they saw each other after the break, she was going to have to tell him how she felt and let the cards fall as they may.

CHAPTER 9:

New Beginnings

Beginnings are sudden, but also insidious. They creep up on you sideways, they keep to the shadows, they lurk unrecognized. Then, later, they spring.
-Margaret Atwood

The two-week Christmas break offered a natural opportunity for Jade and Leo to have a break away from each other. Jade was visiting Nick and Lisa and he was visiting his father. Leo sent Jade several text messages while they were apart, but he really missed her.

Leo was very attracted to her, and he was reasonably sure that she had feelings for him too, but after the break, if she wasn't ready to deal with it yet, Leo would try to be patient a little while longer.

He came back from two weeks of visiting with his father, determined to get closer to Jade. Leo had an idea.

Leo opened Jade's classroom door Friday afternoon and offered a tentative smile, "Want to go to a hockey game?"

"Professional hockey?"

"Absolutely! The Nashville Predators play there. I have tickets for next Saturday night. Do you want to go?"

"Well, I'm from Chicago, Blackhawks territory, so I'm not sure I could break my loyalty."

"Aww, come on. It's not like they're playing the Hawks. Your loyalties will remain unchallenged."

"Well, I guess I could go," she replied grudgingly, "How much do I owe you for the ticket?"

"You can get the next one," he offered, "Listen. The game starts at 7:00 pm, but we should probably leave at about 2:00 pm because it takes about three hours to get there and we can have dinner beforehand. Sound ok to you?"

"You mean miss out on all the quality junk food at the arena?" She asked, smiling.

He shook his head, laughing. "I swear, you have the worst eating habits of any woman I have ever met," He reflected.

"What's wrong with ice cream, granola bars, and taco chips?" She asked in mock seriousness.

"Not a thing—as long as you eat something more nutritious sometimes, too."

She nodded in reply, "Whatever. So what did you have in mind?"

"That's classified. You'll find out next Saturday night."

"Ok, should I come over to your house or meet you here?"

"I'll come to your place."

"See you then." Leo said with a wide smile and exited her classroom.

Jade stared at her classroom door, watching him walk across the hall, back to his classroom. She turned and leaned over to grab her messenger bag from under her desk and felt a blush rise in her cheeks. Jade really didn't want to be this nervous about going out with Leo.

He had become such an important part of her life. Leo had been making sure she made it to lunch every day. He mostly sat back and ate while she talked to other faculty members. But, Leo had crept inside Jade's defenses. He made her feel something she had never felt before and even though Jade was 99% sure that Leo was interested in more than just friendship with her she was still nervous about risking losing his companionship. He had gotten under her skin and that scared the hell out of her. She couldn't imagine her going back to her life before him. But, Jade wasn't sure how to tell Leo that she had feelings for him.

Leo knew that he should have been honest about the fact that he bought the hockey tickets specifically because he knew that she loved hockey. He liked the idea of watching her get charged up. She needed to relax and have some fun, and he wanted to help her do both. The fact that it also made him feel better was something Leo refused to worry about.

Leo wanted to be more than her friend and co-worker, but he recognized the vulnerability in Jade. She was in transition; still recovering from the grief of losing her family and adjusting to a new life as a teacher in a new place. She was just beginning to live again, and he wanted to be there, along for the ride, right beside her.

The day of the game, Jade had woken up earlier than usual, feeling unaccountably edgy. She tried to brush the restless feeling aside by taking a long walk but when she came home, she noticed that it was still only 9:00 am and Leo wasn't due to pick her up for the hockey game until 2:00 pm. "Argh! I'm so pathetic," she growled out loud at her own silly feelings of nervousness. Trying to pull herself together, she's startled when the phone rings.

"Hello."

"This is Maddie. What are you up to?"

"Not a thing right now. Why?"

"Can you come over? I'll make you lunch. I just saw my son's progress report and he's failing math."

"Yeah, actually you picked a great time. I don't have to be anywhere for a few hours."

"Great! Do you know where I live?"

"No, give me your address."

After she told her the address and gave her directions, Jade let her know that she would jump in the shower and be over in about an hour.

Jade arrived at the large, white farm house where Maddie lived. The house was on a large plot of land but the home itself had fallen into disrepair. A cute little boy with short dark hair and freckles sat up in a huge oak tree in front of the house when Jade pulled up. He called down to Jade.

"Hey, are you her friend? The teacher?"

"Yes, my name is Jade. You're Dakota, right?" The boy nodded his head and jumped out of the tree in front of her.

"I hate math and I'm stupid. Tell her, okay."

Jade looked at him. "Did you try your best?"

"I get the answers right, but I don't do it the way the teacher wants."

"So what's the problem?"

"I don't know how to do what she wants me to do. It doesn't make sense. So even though I get the right answer, it's still wrong."

"I think I can help you figure this out, but if I do, you have to make me a promise."

"There's always a catch."

"So…?"

"Alright, what's the deal?"

"Don't call yourself stupid."

"Fine."

"Do you have any of your work I can see?"

He shrugged his shoulders.

"Let's go talk to your mom. I don't want her to think I forgot about you."

When Jade turned to walk to the house, she saw Maddie watching them from the kitchen window. They walked in together and Maddie looked at Jade expectantly.

"I like your house."

"Thanks. It's my dad's. He's away a lot, being a pilot."

"Wow, I didn't even know there was an airport nearby."

Maddie laughed. "Not that kind of pilot. He steers a riverboat."

"Wow. I guess I should know that by now. In Chicago, we don't really think about rivers being commercially important anymore. Rivers are used mostly for tourism and recreation."

"I will have you know that over one hundred twenty-five million tons of coal and other commodities are moved down the Mississippi river on average each year. Thousands of people's livelihoods are dependent on rivers. Sorry, my father is always talking about life on the river."

Dakota stood in the doorway, waiting.

Jade spoke first. "Dakota, you want to show me what you're working on."

"I'll go get my books."

Jade followed Maddie into the large dining room. In the center, there was a round oak table. "You can sit here at the table." She watched Dakota go to his room to find his backpack. "I really appreciate this. He just gets so defensive. I can't even talk to him."

"Honestly, I think he just has a misunderstanding with the teacher about what she wants but we'll take a look."

"Yeah. Do you want a soda?"

"I'm good, thanks."

"Mom, can I have a soda?"

"Sure."

After about an hour of looking at his homework, Maddie called them to lunch. "Dakota, go wash your hands."

While Dakota washed his hands, Maddie showed her to the kitchen table. "I hope you like chili."

"I do. It smells great, thanks."

"How'd it go?" She whispered.

"I think he's feeling better."

They ate Chili and cornbread while Dakota admitted he felt better about his schoolwork with the help of Jade.

Dakota ate quickly and asked his mother, "Can I go visit Mr. Randall? He said he'd help me make a fort."

She looked uncomfortable for a minute before answering. "Honey, I don't know. You shouldn't be bothering him. I'm sure he has other things he needs to do. I can try to help you."

"Mom, you don't know anything about building stuff. Come on. I promise, he offered to help me."

Maddie sighed. "Oh, alright. Here, take him some cookies, and don't forget to thank him."

"I promise. I'm not a baby, Mom," He replied, slamming the door behind him.

"That's fine, but remember its movie night," Maddie said to the closed door.

"He's at that age. He doesn't have a dad. Well, obviously he has a dad, he's just not in the picture."

"I'm really sorry."

"Well, it hasn't been an issue but I guess they get to a certain age when they start to look for that 'father figure.'"

"It sounds like your neighbor is someone he looks up to."

"I grew up with Alec." She seemed wistful for a moment. "Everything is different, though. Anyhow, thanks again for coming here and helping Dakota. I've just been at a loss for what to do, ya know?"

"No problem at all. I told you to just call if you needed me, and thanks for the chili. Maddie, if you want to talk…"

"Thanks, but I'm good. Do you want to see the house?"

"I think I probably need to go. I'm going out for the day with a friend. How about a rain check?"

"Sure, anytime."

Jade got in her car and sat there for a moment, wondering about Dakota's father and the mystery of Maddie and Alec. It wasn't her business, but she felt bad for Maddie going it alone, she supposed. Jade would just make sure that she was available if and when Maddie needed her.

Jade was nearly home when Leo called.

"How bad would it be if I picked you up a little earlier?"

Jade was just about to ask how early when she turned into her driveway and saw him sitting in front of her house. Instead of responding, she disconnected her phone, running right past him and into her house. Leo started to feel a little silly for showing up early until his phone alerted him to a text.

"Need to change clothes. Be out in 10 minutes."

Jade took fifteen minutes to be exact, but she looked so good in her red sweater and just above the knee corduroy skirt that Leo didn't mind waiting at all.

Leo turned as she opened the passenger side door. "I thought you said 2:00 pm?"

"Well I got an earlier dinner reservation, and we don't want to be late," He responded, sheepishly.

"I went over to help a friend. Her son is having some trouble with math."

"That was nice of you."

"I think she's a bit overwhelmed. I don't know her really well, but I feel like I want to help her however I can."

"You're a nice person." He said reaching across the console between their seats to squeeze her hand.

Neither of them said anything for a minute and then Jade broke the silence.

"Well don't forget that I'm a woman. I need a bathroom break between here and Nashville."

"I think I can accommodate you on that." Leo replied, turning the radio down.

"So what are we listening to?" Jade asked, looking towards him.

"Well I have satellite radio so there are a lot of choices, but I guess I'm kind of an old school rock &roll kind of guy. What about you? I've heard lots of different kind of music coming out of your room." He inquired.

"I like everything but country, but I have a soft spot for 80's music and blues."

"Well I have just the station for you, then," Leo said as he adjusted the satellite radio station.

They talked about students, other staff members, and strangely there were no awkward pauses for the whole three hour journey, but he never would reveal where they were going to eat until they finally parked. They got out of the truck and walked around the corner to a seafood restaurant, where he opened the door for her. "I hope you like seafood," he quipped.

Not only was the food good, but the servers did little dance routines at intervals to the music on the jukebox. Jade was really delighted that he had thought to bring her to such a fun place and found herself smiling at Leo as he smiled back at her. It certainly did strange and exciting things to her. She hoped her face wasn't turning beet red.

"It's warm in here."

"Yeah, a little bit, I guess. Do you want another beer?"

"Better not. Actually, I think I'm going to use the bathroom."

"Well, we can split one if you want."

"Okay. I'll be back in a minute."

Once she finished, she saw her waitress at the sink washing her hands. "You're really lucky. I wish my boyfriend looked at me like that."

"Actually, we're just friends. We work together."

"Keep telling yourself that."

Jade felt self-conscious when she rejoined the table. Leo, however, acted just the same as he always did so she quickly shook off the awkward feeling. She had also learned that Leo paid the check while she was gone.

"That's not fair. You got the hockey tickets."

"I told you, next time you can pay."

She rolled her eyes in response and took a sip of his beer. "Okay," she replied after she set the bottle down, "Thank you, Leo."

Leo enjoyed the hockey game. The Predators played well and beat the other team but that's not what he liked about the game. It was the enthusiasm he observed as he watched Jade watching the game. She chanted along with the crowd as though she was a season ticket holder. He found her enthusiasm intoxicating.

She cheered and jeered along with the crowd and shook him after every successful play and point scored, and that had been the point of taking her to the game—to get closer. She had acted a little strangely when they were at the concession stand. She'd seemed to see someone in the crowd, but when he asked her about it, Jade quickly shook it off.

When the game was over, Leo and Jade stopped on the way back to the parking lot at a bar that boasted Karaoke. The bar was crowded and they both had a beer as they watched people make fools of themselves up on the small stage, singing former hits off key as though they were in a competition for a Grammy award. Jade and Leo were sitting at the bar facing the stage where it was warm. Jade became more and more aware of how close Leo was to her. He had his thigh pressed against hers and his arm stretched around the back of her chair. Jade caught his familiar clean, vaguely musky scent from time to time when either one of them moved in their seats. She felt like giving in and sinking into him. She started to stir, suddenly uncomfortable at his proximity. Just then a slightly tipsy older woman came off the stage and thrust a microphone in Leo's face.

"Come on," the patron urged. "Let's hear a song, gorgeous." Jade started to laugh—fully expecting him to hand the microphone back but was startled when he started to sing the Billy Ocean 80's classic, *Loverboy*. What shocked Jade the most was that Leo was singing the words without referring to the prompter and he was staring right at her as he sang. At the beginning of the song, his gaze sparkled with humor, but when he got to the lines, '*And I want you really but the thing is-there's nothing I can say-to stop you from running away.*' Jade felt her face grow warm and her skin seemed to heat up as his eyes burned into her.

Jade itched to touch him, but she was rooted to the spot by his magnetic gaze. In that moment, his stare seemed to burn through her, but the moment passed and his eyes regained their previous lighthearted warmth. After Leo finished the song, he turned off the microphone, handed it to one of the bouncers and returned to her side.

He whispered in Jade's ear, "Getting tired?" She felt slightly dazed so she just nodded, following him out of the steamy bar, hand in hand.

They didn't try to speak again until they were back out on the still crowded street. She still felt a little stunned as she said, "Well that was fun."

Leo looked at her questioningly for a moment before informing her, "The truck is just over on the next block. Let's go."

They walked down Broadway to the parking lot holding hands. When they reached the truck, he opened her door and watched her get in. He closed it and came around and opened his door and sat next to her, but before he started the truck, he picked up her left hand and kissed it, "Did you have fun?"

"I truly had the best time. I can't remember when I just let loose and enjoyed being out, so thank you, Leo. I really needed this, and I couldn't think of anyone else that I would have had a better time with," before she kissed his cheek.

"It was my pleasure. Feel free to crash out if you want. I'll get you home in no time." She nodded her head and stretched across his seat onto his folded jacket that rested next to him. Jade fell asleep to Leo stroking her hair.

Jade barely remembered Leo waking her after the long drive home. The game hadn't ended until after ten, and since they'd stopped at the bar for a bit, it was about 2:00 am before she got to her house. Leo had told her to text when she woke up because he wanted to take her somewhere. She agreed and once she woke up the next morning. He took her for a hike at the nearby Shawnee National Forest and told her about, *The Trail of Tears*.

"After the Indian Removal Act, Native tribes were forced to vacate lands and relocate. The Cherokee that resisted were put in stockades, their homes and belongings were looted. Finally, they were required to travel, mostly on foot, twelve hundred miles. Five thousand Cherokee died on the journey from disease or starvation."

"That's so awful. I can't imagine the U.S. government doing something so horrible. On the other hand, I suppose there are lots of other examples."

"It's not the government per say, just good old fashioned greed. People want things and they see someone else has it, so they form a rationale to take it away from them."

"That's true. It's still horrible, though."

"Yeah, it is."

They talked some more before deciding to return to Leo's truck.

"Have you ever been on a bike—a motorcycle?"

"No, why?"

"I think you would love it. There's no feeling in the world like it. Not this time of year, obviously, it's too cold, but in the spring, when it warms up, I'll take you for a ride."

"Sounds great. I would love to."

Jade liked that he was thinking about the future even though she wouldn't let herself think that far ahead. They had taken to holding hands more and more, and at times, she felt sure that they were more than friends, but other times she worried that she was letting her imagination get away with her.

On one hand, she was thrilled to be Leo's friend. He was funny, kind and generous, not to mention, incredibly good looking. Jade had become so uncomfortable with her attraction to him that she had a hard time looking directly at him. As much as Jade loved spending time with him, she was nearly at the point where she had to either confront him or avoid him altogether. She had some decisions to make, and soon.

The moment of truth came the weekend before Spring Break. Jade went over to his house after work for pizza and a movie, but when she pulled up at Leo's house, she sat in her car and just stared at his perfect cabin that she always hated to leave.

After a few minutes, Leo walked out to her car. He opened her door and said quizzically, "Hey, Beautiful, everything okay? Pizza's already here so why don't you come inside?"

"Leo, I don't think I can do this."

He took in her expression and spoke quietly. "What's wrong, Jade? What can't you do?"

In answer, Jade got out of the car and closed the distance between them, pulling his head down to put her lips to his. She leaned back and looked into his surprised face, "I know we're friends – I like being friends – and I've been trying to keep myself from getting too attached to you, but I have to say that, well, I've failed miserably." She started to turn around but he put his hand on her shoulders and faced her.

Leo's gray eyes stared intently into her dark green ones for a minute and then he clarified, "Well since we're making confessions, I have to confess that I've wanted you since that first day that I charged into your classroom. To be honest, I was kind of hoping that as much as I like being friends, maybe you might come to feel more for me." Neither said anything as they just stared at one another. "So do you want some pizza?" She shook her head and pulled his lips back to hers. What had been at the start an uncertain embrace, quickly turned molten. Leo took control of the kiss and before she knew it, he had backed her into the car.

They tore at each other's clothes, restlessly searching for bare skin. After several minutes of breathless exploring, Leo had his hands on Jade's rear end, "Let's go inside." She took a deep breath and let him help her down to the ground. He leaned his forehead into hers and closed his eyes delicately tracing the planes of her face with his agile fingers as he regained his composure.

Once they were in the house, he led them both into the bedroom and urged her across his lap. She touched his face with the sides of her fingers, tracing his high cheekbones. He moved into her touch and closed his eyes as she laid gentle kisses along the side of his cheek, his neck, and then she freed his hair from the leather ponytail sheath and felt the silky strands run through her fingers. She thought she heard him growl before he stood up with her still in his lap and turned to lay her down with him on top of her.

"Before we go any further, I don't want any more secrets between us. I want us to be out in the open. You okay with that?"

"Yes."

"That's all I needed to hear."

She began unbuttoning his plaid flannel shirt and he shrugged it off absentmindedly to the floor and kicked his shoes off.

He chuckled, "Take it easy. We have all the time in the world."

"Sorry," she murmured.

Leo said warmly, "Don't be."

She slowly began to unbutton her cardigan and he stilled her hands and took over for her, pulling her sweater off and then her blouse, pausing to stare as he unfastened her bra, whispering, "You are so beautiful."

He reached over and traced along the tops of her shoulder blades and down the sides of her arms, easing her lacy bra off her shoulders and discarding it to the floor with the other clothes. He felt his touch raise goose bumps along his path. "I want to make you feel good. Just tell me what you want."

"I want you to touch me and I want to touch you."

He trailed his fingertips slowly to her left breast and began to tease her nipple as he stared into her eyes intently.

"Good?" He asked her.

In answer, she moaned.

She reached for the back of his head and pulled him towards her for a searing kiss. He offered no resistance. They quickly began creating heat from their contact, hastily getting each other's underwear and pants off. When they were both naked, they just laid there staring at each other. Jade trailed her hand along the muscles of his stomach and began to go lower before he stopped her from reaching his erection.

"It's probably better if you don't go there yet. It's been awhile." He said through clenched teeth.

"So I shouldn't do this," She said, tracing the head of his cock with her thumb, giving him a wicked smile.

Leo growled and rolled on top of her before she was able to touch him again. He began trailing his lips and tongue down her chest, stomach, and then her inner thighs as he rubbed the sides of her rear. He looked up at her in question before he gently separated her thighs wider, laying more slow kisses closer to her center as he looked up at her with hooded eyes.

"You said you wanted touching, right?"

She quickly licked her lips and tried to say yes but her mouth was dry, so no sound escaped.

He put his index finger into her center and felt her wetness. He then added another finger and gently blew against her. She began to squirm and he heard her moan.

"How about if I taste you—would that be okay?"

"Yes," She hissed through clenched teeth.

He dipped his head and took a taste as he continued to tease her with his fingers. As her moans became more fevered, he held her legs wider as he moved to take her fully into his mouth. He worried her clit until she came apart, but still he continued to lick and tease her until she climaxed again. Once he got every last moan out of her, he then rose up to kiss her, letting her taste herself on his warm tongue. Once she had almost recovered, she tried to stealthily reach her hand down his thick length that was pressed up against his stomach, and he hissed softly.

"Careful, I'm not going to last too long. I don't want to embarrass myself.

She just stared at him for a minute before rolling him onto his back, then slowly moved down his body.

She slid her hands down his body slowly until she reached to trail the tip of her finger up his length. He sucked in a breath and grabbed her wrist to stop her.

"I would love to do more touching, but right now, I would rather make love to you. How does that sound?" Leo enquired his eyes dark and intense.

"Then what are you waiting for?"

He rolled on to his side and reached into his drawer, grabbing a string of condoms.

She laughed "Ah. Good thing you had those on hand, huh?"

"I've wanted you for a long time. I was just waiting for you to be ready."

"I'm glad."

"I haven't been with anyone for a very long time. I didn't want to be until you."

"Well I don't want you to be disappointed. I haven't really been with...well, I'm not experienced."

"Then that is going to make this even better. I'll make it worth it for you."

She kissed him long and slow before she said in his ear, "Show me how to put this on you."

And he did.

Chapter 10:

Love

I fell in love the way you fall asleep: slowly, then all at once.
-John Green

Jade woke up with Leo wrapped around her, and as good as it felt, she needed to get up to go to the bathroom. So with a little maneuvering, she was able to get out from under his grip and made her way to the bathroom in the dark, tripping over their discarded clothes. When she finished and opened the bathroom door, she noticed Leo's shirt on the floor, so she picked it up and brought it up to her nose—he always smelled so good. She put the shirt on and climbed back into his bed, snuggling her back against him as she fell back into a blissful sleep.

When Jade woke again, she was startled to find herself alone in the bed. She walked out into the living room and heard Leo stirring in the kitchen. When she walked into the room there was Leo with his long hair loose down his back, wearing only a pair of pale blue cotton pyjama pants. His back was facing her at the stove as he made pancakes. She came in slowly behind him and put her arms around his bare waist, placing her cheek against the back of his neck and closed her eyes.

"Something smells good," Jade murmured, "and the pancakes don't smell bad, either."

"Hi there. How did you sleep?" He asked as he turned around, putting his arms around her waist.

"Are you kidding?" Jade smiled into his chest and then looked up, "Never better. How about you?"

In answer, he nuzzled her neck and quickly kissed her. "Mmm. I'll tell you all about it later. Sit down and have some pancakes."

They ate together quietly. Once they were finished, Leo picked up their plates, put them in the sink and took her hand, leading her into the living room. He then sat down on the couch and pulled her next to him, holding her close.

"It's Sunday. We don't have to go anywhere, so stay with me." He said, with a hint of longing.

She turned her face into his chest and said, "This is going to be tricky—working together and being together."

He took a minute to enjoy feeling her lips against his chest and then pulled her to face him. "I know it may be awkward at first, but we can do this. Everything is the same, just better."

"I haven't really been in a relationship before. This is really all new for me."

"We're in this together. Talk to me and tell me what you're thinking."

"I don't want to lose you. We're friends. I haven't really gotten close to anyone in a long time, except for Nick and Lisa, but never with a man." Jade looked at him and stated plainly, "Leo, I feel like the people I care about will either walk out on me or die."

"I'm right here, and I'm not going anywhere. You're not getting rid of me, especially now that I finally have you. Everything is good. Let's relax and let this play out the way it's supposed to. In the meantime, I suggest we take it easy, enjoy being together today and watch some TV." When she seemed to calm down, he kissed her on the nose and slid back on the couch with her in his arms. "Okay, how about watching something funny?" He offered, "Let's see what's on cable."

They couldn't find anything they wanted to watch so they turned to his DVD collection, settling on Harry Potter. They both talked throughout the movies, having both seen them many times. They talked about movies and books and the characters they liked best in both. It helped to ease some of the nervousness in their new status as lovers, but it was a deepening of the intimacy that had been building since they met.

By the time they finished watching the second Harry Potter instalment, they began to realize that they were still partially dressed from the night before.

"I should probably go home. I don't have any clean clothes." She reflected, standing up, not looking forward to the prospect of leaving.

"Well then let's go get you something to wear." He agreed.

"It's probably better if I just go home." She countered awkwardly.

"Do you want to go home?"

She didn't answer, so Leo put his arms around her and spoke softly.

"I don't want you to leave, and if you don't want to either, we could just run over to your house and get your clothes. You could leave for work with me Monday morning."

"Okay, but I can't go like this. I'll go get dressed."

"I like seeing you in my shirt, but you're right. You probably need to go and get something else on in case we get a flat tire or something. Don't want the town to see my girl half naked in only my shirt." He said, but with a big smile on his face.

They dressed and drove together to her house. When they pulled up, they didn't notice the truck parked on the road across from her house. As much as they were oblivious to his presence, he was keenly aware of them and the way they held hands as they walked together in the waning sunlight.

Joe had been fired from his job after hitting Diana with the company's truck. They didn't know about the incident, but when he returned the truck damaged, they'd jumped at the opportunity to get rid of him. His boss had talked to him about his temper, telling him, "I used to be kind of a hot head. I was mad at the world, but it took my first wife walking out on me to get the help I needed."

Screw that.

That blow-hard didn't know shit about being in rehab for months—having to learn how to do everything all over again, having your girlfriend and other people blow you off because you're 'angry.' They had tried to get him to take medication and go to therapy, but how was talking about his feelings going to change the fact that his brain was scrambled.

It couldn't take away the memory problems or the fact that even his own mother acted like she was afraid of him, but oh well; forget all of them. Joe didn't need that job anyway. It was about time he moved on, and moving on was just what he was going to do.

Chapter 11:

Changes

I still don't know what I was waiting for...I turned myself to face me.
-David Bowie

Jade nearly saw the piece he had been painting but as always, Leo turned it away before she could get a glimpse.

"Hey."

Leo shook his head and put his brushes down, "Not ready to be seen yet. Sorry."

She scowled but quickly let it go. She wouldn't take in personally. "Mr. Blackbird, do you have a moment?" Jade asked in a teasing voice.

"Why yes, Ms. Davis. I think that I do. What can I help you with?"

"I was just wondering if you mind me moving your stapler over here?"

"Are you making fun of me?"

"I would never do that, but I think that it looks better here on the bookshelf, next to the pencil sharpener."

"Don't tease me or you'll be sorry."

Jade picked up the stapler and attempted to move it to the bookshelf, but before she had a chance to put it down, Leo snatched it back and returned it to its proper place on his desk. She tried to grab it back, but he pinned her hands above her in one of his and was just about to kiss her when they heard a knock on the door.

Rose wore a broad smile when opened the door and came into Leo's classroom. "Careful guys, you're about to set off the smoke detectors. "Leo released her hands slowly, not looking at all sorry, while Jade's face turned bright red. "Oh, don't be embarrassed. There aren't any kids around, and it's not like it's a surprise. You guys look great together."

Leo smiled, "Thanks, Rose. Listen, I'm not trying to get rid of you, but do you need something?"

"I was looking for Jade, actually. I just wanted to see if you were going to Karate tonight? I thought maybe we could drive together. We could take my car."

"You go ahead," He encouraged her, "I have a few things to finish here without you trying to move my office supplies and distract me. I could come pick you up later if you want? I've been meaning to check it out, actually."

"That sounds like a plan. So when are you going to show me what you're working on?"

Leo turned guiltily away, "You'll just have to be patient, woman. Have fun at Karate. I'll pick you up at 7:00 pm."

"Whatever."

Rose opened the door and held it for Jade, "You guys are so cute."

Jade just smiled and grabbed her bag out of her classroom and they drove together in Rose's car.

"I'm happy for you and jealous as hell. Leo is gorgeous and a really nice guy. He was always kind of quiet before."

"Quiet?"

"Well not quiet, exactly. It was more like reserved, but since you've been here, he's seemed happy."

Her friend's words warmed her, but Jade was also a little nervous about what they meant. She wanted to be optimistic about her feelings for Leo, but it was all so new and unfamiliar, so she decided to change the subject.

"Well what about you? You haven't really talked about anyone. No boyfriend?"

"Nah, my love life at the moment is confined to romance novels. Lately, I've been reading military romance. Love a man in uniform."

"There's somebody for everybody, Rose. You might even find a soldier."

"Sure, don't worry about me. It's just weird at the holidays. Everybody seems to be paired off, and my mother? Don't get me started. Let's just say that I don't have to worry about being single. She does it for me."

"Leo's father is coming to visit for Spring break."

"That's great. Are they close?"

"I guess so. I gather that he's a pretty impressive guy. I suppose I'm about to find out."

"It would seem so. Wow. I guess you guys are pretty serious. Makes sense, though."

"I don't know about being serious. It's not like his father is coming specifically to meet me. They just haven't seen each other in awhile, that's all.

"Okay, Jade. Not pushing, promise."

"I didn't mean to be defensive, either. Sorry. This is just all new to me so I don't have any real answers for you, I guess. I tell you what, let's just go punch something."

"Dad's going to be flying in tomorrow. We'll have to go to Nashville to get him in the morning, but we can still sleep in."

"So do we have a plan for the week? I can't believe how fast this school year has gone. Its spring break, already."

"I don't know. Normally we don't even get together in the spring. It's hard for him to get away for the few days we're off. It will be good to see him, but it makes me wonder. I've been trying to talk him into moving over here. Maybe he's actually looking into it."

"That would be great, Leo. I can't wait to meet him." Jade said excitedly, yet silently terrified.

"We can take him into Paducah and have a nice dinner. Walk around downtown a bit, maybe. There are some galleries I've been meaning to check out. Have you been to the flood wall?"

"I've never been to Paducah."

"Well then, we need to fix that. Paducah is a great city, and small. A lot of artists come there because they have an Artist Relocation Program that gives free gallery space to artists in exchange for fixing it up."

"That sounds good. I went to a gallery crawl in Chicago with my mother once. That's when I had my first glass of champagne."

"I'm not sure that this will be on the same scale as Chicago, but..."

"I'd rather see your work, but I guess I'll settle for other local artists."

"I promise I'll let you see what I'm working on, just not yet." Leo said, kissing her forehead.

"In theory, we could probably spend the night apart sometime," Jade said, cuddling into him.

"I suppose you're right, but why would we?" He asked, wrapping his arms more tightly around her.

"I love your tattoo," She said, tracing the outline with her fingers, "Why two wolves?"

"There's a Cherokee Legend about two wolves. An old Cherokee grandfather told his grandson about a terrible fight going on inside of him between wolves. *"One is evil; full of anger and other negative emotions; the other one is good, full of joy peace and love.'"* He told him, 'that same fight is going on inside of you, and inside of every other person. His grandson asked, *"Which one will win?"* And his grandfather answered, *"The one you feed."*

"I love that. I think we had a very different experience growing up. I'm Irish. My parents were both lapsed Catholics. Even though I was an only child until I was nine, the whole neighborhood always got together for holidays and birthdays. They had barbecues in the summer and potlucks in the colder weather. Everyone on the block was in each others' business. It was nice, but a little overwhelming. I've always been shy."

"That's how it was on the reservation. Everyone was over for every birthday, school holiday. My aunts were so embarrassing. They were *always* in my business, especially after my mom got sick, so I guess we're not so different." Leo observed, gently running his hand under the hem of his shirt that Jade had worn to bed.

"I'm not very sleepy, Leo." Jade said, turning around to face him.

Leo laid back as Jade slowly rolled over and straddled his hips; her eyes half closed in arousal.

Leo answered, his voice suddenly thick with passion, "Me either."

CHAPTER 12:

Giving Thanks: Visitors expected and not…

> *Keeping the door that leads to your heart ajar is destructive as uninvited guests would move in and trample on your feelings, leaving you in great pains, but closing it always is a sure way to spot out the destructive and innovative guest.*
> -Michael Bassey Johnson

"His plane's delayed. The airline sent a notification."

"Oh, then we'll just get lunch and wait, I guess. Leo, what if he doesn't like me?"

"He will. My father is a very smart man and he has excellent judgment. He's going to love you, Jade."

"Hmm. Well it's going to be several hours, so do you want to go into Nashville? We could walk around for awhile."

"Or we could get a hotel room. How many hours do we have?"

Jade turned red and laughed. "We have four hours, but I really don't want to be all…well you know…when I first meet your dad."

"Why not? Sounds good to me. Actually, four hours isn't nearly long enough for what I'm thinking of." He said, squeezing her thigh before lifting his finger upwards under her sweater and into the waistband of her jeans.

"Leo…" She said in a moan.

"I can't help it. You're so incredibly sexy that I can't keep my hands off you. I just want to kiss and lick every little part of you."

"Well then, maybe a hotel isn't such a bad idea after all."

Leo pulled over at the next exit and registered for a room at the first hotel he saw. He and Jade were kissing and pulling at each other's clothes before they even closed the door.

"How long do you think we'll be delayed?"

"Sir, I'm really not sure. There's a huge storm in the Northeast. It came in faster than anyone anticipated, and all those delays are causing problems everywhere."

An attractive woman with short, pale blonde hair and blue eyes walked up to the customer service desk before Ben could turn away. "Excuse me. I have to be in Nashville by 8:00 am tomorrow. Are we getting out of here soon?"

"Ma'am, as I've just told this gentleman. I will make an announcement as soon as I have more information."

"Sounds like a 'no' to me." Greta muttered under her breath.

Ben sat in the only available seat in the waiting area directly across from her, watching as she rifled through her bag for her cell phone, watching her as unobtrusively as he could. She looked so frustrated as she apparently sent a message on her phone, and then stared out of her window.

"This is why I prefer to drive." Ben offered.

"Yeah, me too… I thought this would be faster."

"Too bad we can't just get a refund and drive ourselves."

"My car's at home. I got a ride to the airport."

"Well I'll see what the airline says. I don't want to come back again in the morning."

The announcement came quickly, that due to widespread delays in the East, all flights for the evening were cancelled.

The customer service agents began handing out hotel vouchers.

Ben rose and gathered his carry-on luggage, just as Greta tapped him on the shoulder, "Sir, any chance...could I drive with you? I know you don't know me, but—"

Ben raised his hand to quiet her, "I would be glad to give you a ride to Nashville. My name is Ben."

"Hello, Ben. My name is Greta, and I really appreciate this."

"I can't believe we waited so long. I will never get enough of you."

"I agree," Leo said, laying gentle kisses across her brow, cheeks and lips."When he started to deepen the kiss, Jade pushed him away.

"Wait a minute. What time is it? Your dad!"

"I'll see if I can call him—don't move."

Jade laughed and rolled over.

"Hi Dad. Yeah, we heard you were delayed...What?" He said, sitting up quickly. Jade wrapped the sheet around herself and sat up next to him, "I don't understand, Dad. Why would you drive when you have a plane ticket? Seriously? Who is she? Are you sure? Well don't worry about us. We'll just get a hotel room and wait, I guess. Just be safe and I'll talk to you soon." Leo said as he hung up the phone and kissed Jade on the shoulder.

"What's going on?"

"The plane was delayed overnight so he's driving himself and some woman he's just met."

"You're kidding, right?"

"No, I wish I was."

"Well I'm sure it'll be alright. I mean, you said that he has good judgment, right? If he offered to bring her, he must know what he's doing."

"I guess. I wish he'd called before he left the airport."

"Maybe she was pretty. Your father is widowed, you know."

"I don't know. You would have to know my dad. He doesn't date."

"He's been alone a long time."

"I guess we'll find out when he gets here in about five hours."

Jade smiled, "What will we do until then?"

"I have a few thoughts on that, actually." Leo yanked the sheet off her and pulled her close. They still had a lot more time.

Ben called Leo's cell phone five hours later as he was pulling in to Nashville. Jade and Leo had fallen asleep. He found out their location and pulled in to get his own room so he could get a few hours of sleep also.

They met the next morning for breakfast in a local family restaurant.

"Dad," Leo exclaimed, putting his arm around Jade's waist, "This is Jade."

Ben reached as if to shake her hand but pulled her in for a tight hug instead.

Leo smiled, "It's so good to see you, Dad."

"You too, Leo, and you, Jade."

Leo stepped over and hugged his father after Ben released Jade.

They ordered breakfast and Leo considered his father. "You cut your hair."

"Yes, I did."

"It looks good. It's just unexpected."

"Your aunt convinced me I needed an update."

Their breakfast orders arrived and they were all silent as they descended upon their food.

As they finished up, Leo said to his father, "So you weren't killed by your passenger, I take it?"

Ben looked taken aback for a moment. "No."

Jade watched Ben's expression change from surprised, to wistful, and then to sad. She and Leo exchanged a look.

"It was nice of you to drive her. What was her name, Dad?"

"Greta."

"Sorry we didn't get to meet her."

"Yes." He explained, "She had an appointment. I was coming this way so—"

"Is she going to drive back with you?"

Ben looked out the window while he answered. "No. Greta has to go back tonight. She has a plane ticket."

"So are you planning on seeing her again?"

Leo's father just shook his head.

"Oh. Well, how are we going to do this? We have my truck and yours. We could just leave yours parked here and drive back together."

"That's fine, if you can bring me back to Nashville?"

"Of course, let's go park your truck."

They drove back to Leo's house and made plans for hiking and sightseeing during Ben's stay, but Ben didn't talk much.

"We can take you to the school if you want, Mr. Blackbird. I know you would like to see the work he's doing with his students."

"Of course, but call me Ben, please. Leo, do you have any new pieces?"

"A few things," he said evasively.

"You haven't shown me anything." Jade reminded him.

"Not ready to show it yet."

"Okay, I get that. My mother was always the same way."

"Oh, was your mother an artist, too?" Ben inquires.

"Yes, and an art teacher."

"That's interesting."

"Leo told me you're a furniture designer?"

"Yes. I'm a carpenter, but I make furniture, mostly."

"I would love to see some of your work."

"The company is called A New Life. I use reclaimed wood and other materials."

"Now that sounds really interesting. I like the name, too."

"There are pictures on my website. We can look at them later if you'd like."

"I would, very much."

They spent the rest of the journey discussing Leo's family back in North Carolina. Leo and Ben always managed to keep Jade in the discussion. Once they got back to Leo's house, they showed Ben to the guest room and got him situated, then while Jade went to karate class, Leo showed Ben a couple of the pieces that he was working on that he wasn't ready to show to Jade.

"That's really wonderful, Leo. Have you shown Jade your work?"

"Not yet. I have a couple more pieces I want to add to finish the series."

"So how long have you and Jade been together?"

Leo turned away from the canvas and looked at his father, smiling, "Jade's great, isn't she?"

"Yes, she is. But you still haven't answered my question."

"Well, I guess we've been circling each other since school started, spending time together as friends and co-workers, but we only just started dating. She has some baggage." Leo smiled, "I hadn't done any real painting until August. She's my muse, and I'm a walking cliché."

"Well, I like her very much. She obviously makes you very happy. You chose well, Son."

"What about you, Dad?"

It was Ben's turn to look uncomfortable. "Well, I was seeing someone for a few months but…well, we wanted different things."

"There's someone for everyone."

"Perhaps. How long has she been taking karate lessons?"

"Just a few months, and she loves it. She has her first belt promotion coming in a month. It's helped her become more confident."

Ben nodded his approval but didn't comment.

"Let's start dinner. Jade will be back soon."

Jade was changing clothes after karate when Rose came into the changing room. "You looked good out there. You still liking it?"

"Yeah, I do."

"That's good. What are you doing for the break?"

"Well, Leo's father is in town so I think we'll have dinner at his house."

"Oh, that's right. Is he nice?"

"He is. Listen, I better get back because they're waiting for me. You have a great spring break, Rose."

"You too, Jade."

Jade needed to stop by the convenience store and wasn't surprised to see Maddie working.

"Hey, Jade. How are you?"

"I'm great. How are you?"

"I'm doing much better. I talked to Dakota's math teacher yesterday and he's really improving. I guess whatever you told him did the trick. I owe you."

"Dakota is a really smart kid. He just had to look at his work with a different perspective. On the other hand, I am willing to be rewarded with your chili anytime."

"You have a deal. Maybe you can stop by next weekend? I'll give you that tour, but your soda is on me today."

"Thanks, I appreciate it, Maddie."

"See you later."

Once Jade made it to Leo's, she could smell the pot roast before she even opened the door. Ben and Leo were dressed in sweats and sitting in the kitchen talking when she walked in. She kissed Leo on the forehead.

"Hey, how was karate?" He said, pulling her toward him.

"Great, but I'm really sweaty."

"Jump in the shower. Food is just about done."

She looked at Ben. "Sorry, don't mind me. I'm a mess. Did you get a nap?"

"No, I'll probably just turn in early."

"Then let me jump in the shower and I'll be right back. I'm starved."

"Hurry up, woman. After dinner, we're going to check out Dad's website. It's really impressive."

"Ooh, can't wait."

Jade showered quickly and returned wearing fresh sweat pants and a long sleeved t-shirt. "I'm having a beer. Anyone else?"

"No, we already had a couple. I'm good with water."

"Ben, what can I get you?"

"Tea would be nice."

Jade gets Ben's tea and says, "So what were you two up to while I was gone?"

Leo and his father exchanged a sly smile, "We were just catching up on things back home. You didn't miss anything."

"You showed him your new work, didn't you?"

"I told you, Honey. I'm not ready for you to see it yet." Leo glanced at his father questioningly for a moment before continuing, "I want to finish the series before I show you. I promise that it will all make sense when you see all the pieces together."

"Hmm, I don't know why you're making it such a big secret."

Ben decided to offer up a distraction, "I'm thinking of relocating my company here."

"Really? That's great, Dad, but do you mind me asking why?"

"I'm no longer doing the cabinetmaking. Most of what I sell now is through my website, and I can sell online from anywhere."

"That would be so great." Jade said excitedly.

"Yeah, it would be. When?"

"I'm not sure. I'll have to work out the details."

"Is that why you came to visit?"

"In part, but I wanted to see you, Son. I've also been thinking a change would do me good. It certainly has improved things for you." Ben regarded Jade.

"That's great. Of course you can stay here as long as you like."

"Well, for now I'm only going to be here a few days, but I would need to get my own house with some land so I can build a studio. Hopefully, I can find some land nearby. But in the meantime, why don't we eat. Jade keeps sniffing the air so I think we had better feed her.

After dinner they looked at Ben's website. Jade 'oohed' and 'aahed' over his furniture. Ben also researched homes and land for sale nearby and they made plans to look at a few places the next day. Afterwards, Ben went to sleep in Leo's guest room.

When they had perused Ben's website, Jade found herself fantasizing about what several of the pieces would look like in Leo's house. It terrified her to think of how quickly she had come to care for Leo, but Jade was determined not ruin it by getting ahead of herself. They had only known each other six months after all. Thinking and feeling were completely separate things, and Jade realized that she was already in way over her head.

Chapter 13:

Just When You Thought Things Were Going Well

In the book of life, the answers aren't in the back.
-Charlie Brown

Ben's visit went very well. They looked at a few properties and Ben managed to find a real estate agent that helped him locate a property only a couple of miles away from Leo's house. The house needed work, but Ben put in an offer and went back to North Carolina to make plans to sell his existing space and most of his inventory. Jade and Ben had gotten along great, and she had grown pretty attached. He had Leo's enigmatic charm and kindness. They had even discussed going out to North Carolina to visit him in the meantime.

Jade continued to stay every night at Leo's house. She always meant to go home but she never seemed to end up staying there overnight, so they fell into a pattern of driving to school, then to her house to seek fresh clothes, then back to Leo's. It felt good to be there, but the days of peace didn't last long.

The Friday after spring break Jade acted as one of the chaperones for a field trip to the movie theater. It served as a reward for the students who had been able to go the whole quarter without a write-up. Jade was particularly pleased to note that Kayden had been one of the students included. He had become a lot more cooperative in her class and she had to admit that he'd become one of her favorite students.

After Jade had gotten all the students on the bus and to the theater, she began to relax a little and enjoy the film. It was always a bit nerve-wracking, making sure that all the students who were on the bus were there, especially since she was still getting to know faces and names. The film based on a popular young adult novel and was a little hard to watch with its violence in places was very engaging and the students were clearly captivated. She took the opportunity to go to the bathroom, knowing that the students were safe with the other teachers present to watch them.

Jade had just come out of the bathroom when someone grabbed her from behind, covered her mouth with a large hand and started to drag her toward the side door of the theater, but by some miracle, just then she heard Kayden shout, "Hey let go of her!"

His shouting alerted theater personnel, causing the manager and an usher to go running.

"Let her go! We called the cops!"

Joe hesitated momentarily and then shoved her hard against the wall, running out the side door. Kayden came up behind Jade, "Ms. Davis, are you okay? Who was that guy? Have you seen him before?" He asked anxiously.

She turned around and faced him as she sank to the carpet floor on her rear end. Her face was pale and her hands were shaking. "God Kayden, you saved my life."

"Who was he?" Kayden asked, frantically scanning her from head to toe, "Did he hurt you?"

At that point the manager came over to her with two uniformed police officers. The manager spoke first. "Miss, these officers need to speak to you. Why don't we go back to my office?"

"I'm here with a group of students. I don't want to get separated from them."

The manager told her that they would keep an eye out for them and hold them in the lobby until the interview was finished. Kayden accompanied her since he had witnessed the incident. Jade told the Paducah police the bizarre story of Joe when she still lived up north, as well as her suspicions that he had been stalking her. She explained that this was in part the reason that she had decided to move to southern Illinois. They wrote it all down and told her she would have to come back later to the station to file an order of protection against Joe.

Leo had texted her several times since she arrived at the movie. If she didn't know better, she could swear he sensed something was wrong. Why else would he text her during a movie when he knew she would have her phone off? The texts weren't anything prophetic, just "How's it going?" and "It's quiet back here at the school," and even an "I miss you, so hurry back." She hadn't answered him yet, but she felt better knowing he was thinking of her. She didn't want him to worry and she realized that she needed to tell him about the situation with Joe. It was something she needed to tell him face to face though, not in a text.

Luckily, Jade was done with her interview with the police just before the movie was finished, so she and Kayden sat outside in the lobby waiting. Jade felt grateful that he had intervened, and sorry that her personal life had spilled over into her professional life.

"Thanks for being there. I'm sorry you had to miss the whole movie."

He ignored her apology, "Ms. Davis, for real, who was that guy? Does Mr. Blackbird know about him?"

"No," she replied surprised, then asked wearily, "So does everyone know about me and Mr. Blackbird?"

He answered with a condescending expression, "Yeah. I mean, you guys are always together."

"About today…can we avoid talking about this on the bus? That's not how I want Mr. Blackbird to find out about this. It should come from me."

"I ain't gonna say nothin'," he confirmed. "I'm worried about you, Ms. Davis. What if I wasn't there?" Kayden asked, seriously.

"I will always be grateful that you were."

They stood up as everyone came out of the movie. Most of the students started to file into the bathrooms before they left for the bus ride home. The other teachers looked at her questioningly, so she nodded. Jade turned to the kids who had come out of the bathroom and were now waiting for the rest of the students.

She asked a group of arriving students "Did you like the movie?"

There were murmurs of assent. She started leading them to the bus and Kayden immediately caught up with her and looked around as he matched her stride. When he got on the bus, he hesitated a minute before speaking quietly to her, "Tell Mr. Blackbird. If you were my girl, I would want to know."

Jade was overcome with emotion—taken aback by his insight.

Once all of the students were seated on the bus, Jade sat down and looked at her phone. Rose leaned over the aisle toward her and asked, "What's going on?"

"I'll tell you about it later." She replied.

After a moment of hesitation, she nodded. "Okay."

She looked at the messages again from Leo and texted him back. "I miss you too, and we're on our way back. See you in about forty-five minutes. I'll buy you dinner. We need to talk."

"Everything okay?" Leo quickly texted back.

"It will be when I see you," she replied.

"Okay, can't wait."

Jade stared at her phone and wondered how she was going to get through the next half hour.

Kayden seemed to sense her anxiety because he handed his mp3 over to her and told her, "Here, listen to this."

She listened for a couple of minutes and then took the earphones off, "I like that," she admitted. "Who is it?"

"That's Big Boi," he replied. "I know you must've heard some of his cuts before. That song is really old. He's the lead singer of OutKast," he clarified. "Now listen to this." He continued talking about music. Kayden filled her in about what she didn't know about recent hip-hop and rap. She assured him that she liked R & B, hip-hop, Blues, Rap (mild), Reggae, Classical, and opera, but not country music. The whole musical sojourn, she soon realized, was an effort to help relax her after her scare, and it was surprisingly effective. She couldn't believe how she didn't feel as tense by the time the bus arrived at the school.

Once the bus arrived, Jade made sure everyone got into the building and into the cafeteria to wait for the final end-of-the-day bell. She promised Kayden a pan of brownies for his heroics. At first he seemed to balk at the idea, but common sense prevailed and he accepted her promise of the tangible 'Thank you."

Once the bell rang and the students had scattered en masse toward the buses and exits, Jade walked out of the cafeteria and down the corridor toward Leo's classroom. The panic began to rise in her again at the prospect of telling him about the attack. She made it as far as the Teachers' lounge when he saw her face and rushed over to her.

"Something happened?" he inquired.

"Let's get out of here first," she suggested.

He took her hand, "You're shaking. What the hell is going on?"

"I'll tell you, but let's get out of here first."

"Okay. Give me a minute to grab my bag. Do you need anything out of your room?"

She just shook her head.

Once they got in his truck, she started to speak without looking at him.

"Before I moved down here, my friends Nick and Lisa, I told you about them, they introduced me to this guy. His name was Joe, and he was the brother of a friend of Nick's. Anyway, they were always worried because I didn't go out, so they figured they would set me up. Well, he turned out to be really weird. He ignored me the night I met him and I got a strange feeling about him. Then he asked me out and I told him I wasn't interested. He didn't take it too well.

I had the feeling he was following me before I moved down here. It was part of the reason I decided to leave, actually, and now it appears he's found me and followed me here."

She took a deep breath and looked into her lap before she continued. Leo sat looking at her, patiently listening.

"He tried to grab me at the movie theater. I mean, he did grab me when I was coming out of the bathroom. If Kayden hadn't been there to stop him…"

"Thank God you're okay. I've got you now," Leo confirmed as he pulled her to him. She could tell that he was trying to keep himself steady for her, and that meant a lot to her, especially right now when she just needed him to hold her.

He pulled her tight to his chest and let his own panic rise. What if that psycho had gotten her? How was he going to protect her? He was determined that he wouldn't let her out of his sight again until the asshole was caught. The first step they needed to take was to go to her house and clear it out. She definitely didn't need to be there alone, not that she'd been spending much time there anyway. He didn't want to be a pushy jerk, but surely she would understand the need to stay with him while this guy was loose.

He wiped his shirtsleeves over her wet cheeks and waited for her to face him. "Why don't we swing by your place and pick up some of your clothes. I don't think it's a good idea for you to be alone until this bastard is caught, okay?" She nodded and shook her head, pulling away to put on her seat belt. He started to drive, heading toward her house.

Leo continued, "Hopefully he'll disappear now that he knows people are looking for him. He took a hell of a chance trying to grab you in broad daylight. I think we need to stay close," he stated simply.

Jade didn't say anything. She just looked out of the passenger side window, expressionless as they continued to drive toward her house.

"I thought this was over with." She finally murmured, her head pressed against the glass of the window.

He grabbed her hand in the now dark truck cab and brought her palm to his mouth.

When they pulled up in front of her house, Jade looked around uneasily. She had felt safe up until this afternoon, but one afternoon had changed all of that. She needed to call Nick and Lisa and tell them what was happening.

They walked to the door of Jade's house and froze. Someone had spray painted "BITCH" on her door. Leo pulled out his phone and called 911.

"It's not an emergency," she said weakly.

"The hell it isn't! First the psycho tries to grab you, and now this," he countered. "Hello, I need a patrol car to come to 12200 Crescent Drive. I want to report an act of vandalism at my girlfriend's house. She was attacked in Paducah earlier today and the Paducah police have already talked to her, but the point is that this is clearly the same guy." He paused, listening to the voice at the other end of the phone. "Yeah, we'll wait inside." He disconnected the call and then turned to her. "Let's go in. I'll pack your clothes."

"I'll do it." She said, trying to sound like she wasn't about to fall apart.

Leo shook his head and paced the room. "I can't just stand here. I feel so helpless. God, what if he had hurt you?" He said, looking like he wanted to punch the wall.

Jade came up behind him and put her arm around his waist. Leo grabbed her tight for a minute then spun her around and kissed her desperately. He led her backward toward the kitchen wall and he frantically unbuttoned her white cotton blouse and discarded it along with the black wool cardigan over it. He brought his mouth to the lacy cups of her white demi-bra. "I can't lose you," he said as he shoved her bra strap down, uncovering her left breast. Jade sucked in her breath and gasped as he took her nipple into his mouth. After a blissful moment, he pulled his mouth away from her breast and told her more sternly, "I'm not going to lose you," before he claimed her mouth with his.

He quickly lowered his pants and hers and buried himself inside of her. Her back was against the wall, supported by his strong hands. They never lost eye contact—the moment was too intense. The feelings were too raw and unspoken. She was his, and he would fight heaven and hell to keep her safe.

Chapter 14:

Protective Instincts

> *In art as in love, instinct is enough.*
> -Anatole France

Thank God for slow police response. Leo and Jade managed to get their clothes back on before the police arrived. While she was talking to the police, Leo pulled out her suitcases and began throwing the contents of her dresser drawers into the bags. He then started pulling the clothes on hangers over to the couch, laying them flat. He went underneath the sink and pulled out a couple of garbage bags and went back to her closet again. Jade excused herself from the officer.

"Leo, what are you doing?" She whispered to him.

"I'm getting your shoes. Oh my God, woman. How many pairs do you have?"

"We don't have to get absolutely everything."

"Might as well."

"I'm not moving in with you. This is temporary."

"Temporary? We'll talk about it later." Leo said, patronizingly.

Jade noticed the officer looking impatient and finally answered, "Fine, but we will talk about this later." She could have sworn she heard him mutter something like "stubborn woman" as she walked away, but she wasn't sure.

Jade went back to the police officer as Leo continued throwing all of her shoes into the garbage bag and hauled it over to the couch. Finally, the police officer finished his report and left.

"Anything else you need to bring. I mean it's not like you can't come back over here, but I definitely don't want you coming back by yourself."

"I think that's it. I have my jewelry in my bag."

"Let's go then. We might have to make more than one trip."

They carried her things out and together it took the both of them two trips to his truck to get it all. She laughed as she slid into the passenger seat.

"Where were you when I packed to come down here?"

"I was down here waiting for you," He turned and murmured into her hair.

Jade reached over to kiss him. "Let's get out of here. I hate that he's been here, for who knows how long, watching me. For all I know, he could be watching me right now."

"Well, he'll have to come through me to get you."

"Don't say that. I couldn't stand it if anything happened to you."

"Then you know how I feel. Let's go home."

He started the truck and drove off into the darkness. On the way to Leo's, she reluctantly called Nick to let him know the latest with Joe. She called him through his truck's Bluetooth.

Nick answered her phone call on the second ring, "Hey, Beautiful, how are you? We miss you."

Jade smiled, but emotion strained her voice, "I miss you guys too. I have some news. Joe showed up today."

"What? No way, I can't believe it. Are you sure it was him?" He asked, quickly.

"I didn't just see him. He grabbed me and tried to drag me out of a movie theater. I was chaperoning a group of school kids. If one of the kids didn't show up in time, he would've dragged me right out of there. If that wasn't bad enough, when we came back to my apartment to get my clothes, someone, and I'm assuming it was him, spray painted "BITCH" on my door." She choked out in a voice thick with emotion. Tears began to fall silently down her cheeks and Leo unbuckled Jade's seat belt and urged her over in the bench seat, pulling her to him.

Nick said in a raspy voice, "Jesus. What a nightmare. There's something I didn't tell you."

She could hear Lisa in the background, asking what he meant, "I heard from Al, Joe's brother. It seems that he had a car accident. I guess it was pretty bad and there was an issue with an ex-girlfriend. That's all he knew."

Lisa spoke before Jade or Leo could respond. "I can't believe you didn't say anything!"

"Honey, I was distracted. That's when we found out about the baby. I'm really sorry. I can't believe we got you into this. I had assumed that after you left, he had gone his own way. We haven't heard anything from him here, and you've never mentioned anything about him bothering you again until now. I just thought he'd let it go and moved on. I'm so sorry, Jade. I would never have introduced the two of you if I had known. I would never want to see you hurt."

She returned quickly, "It's not your fault. You were trying to be a good friend. You had no idea what he was like."

"I know, Sweetie, but I hate that you're a sitting duck down there." Nick said, sadly.

Leo spoke before Jade had a chance, "She's not. Sorry to butt in, but I'm Leo Blackbird and Jade and I…well, I'll make sure she's safe. That's a promise."

"Good to know. Jade is our family."

Jade had told them what they needed to know, so she wanted to change the subject, "Are you feeling any better, Lisa?"

"It's getting better. I'm still tired, but I only threw up once today."

Jade winced, "I guess that's better."

"She's doing great, Jade. Don't worry about us."

"Not possible. I just wanted to keep you in the loop of what happened so you don't get mad when you find out some other way, so I'll call you tomorrow night. Love you guys. "

Nick and Lisa said together, "Love you too, Honey."

Jade disconnected her phone and looked out the window at the dark tree lined highway. She let her mind drift back to the past when she was with Nick and Lisa. They had some happy times, but those were the only good times she had had since her mother and sister died. They were the only family she had left. Jade didn't consider her father family. He hadn't been there for her, leaving her to go through so much by herself. He left them, breaking her mother, and Jade could never forgive him for that.

"Hey, you're a million miles away."

"No, just three hundred and fifty or so."

"You wish you were back there?"

She turned to look at him, surprised by the comment. "No, I just miss them sometimes. Don't you miss your family?"

"Sure, but it's not home anymore."

"That's how I feel. I'm where I want to be."

"That's good, 'He had gotten under her skin and that scared the hell out of her. Cause you're where I want you to be, too."

Jade mumbled under her breath, "I hope you don't change your mind."

He asked, "What?"

She replied, "Nothing."

Leo pulled in front of the house and came around to her side of the truck just as she got out. When she stood up, he put his arms around her waist, pulling her to him so her back was tucked into him as he nibbled softly on her ear and whispered, "I'm not going to get sick of being with you. I don't think that's even possible at this point. Now, let's get you unpacked."

He walked over to the guest bedroom and turned on the overhead light. He turned and took some of her clothes that were on hangers and hung them in the closet and stood to face her, "I thought you could put your clothes in here. Consider it like a walk-in closet where the whole room belongs to your clothes and your hundreds of pairs of shoes."

She turned and faced him her eyes sparkling, "I don't know what to say. How did I get so lucky?"

He smiled broadly and spun her towards the living room, "Hold that thought. Here, let's get the rest of your stuff put away."

They went out to the truck and grabbed the shoe bag and the suitcases and locked the truck up. It only took about half an hour to hang up the rest of her clothes and put away her shoes, then Jade and Leo went to his room, turned out the lights and went to bed. It felt a little awkward at first when they got dressed for bed. Jade was preoccupied with the situation with Joe. She was glad to be with Leo, but it wasn't under the type of circumstances she wanted. Jade was also worried about Joe trying to hurt Leo because of her. She couldn't live with that. Jade put one of Leo's t-shirts on and climbed under the covers. He joined her, wearing a pair of pajama bottoms. Once he crawled into bed, he turned on his elbow to face her and asked her, "Where are you now?"

She looked over at him and answered anxiously, "I'm here. I'm just worried that somebody is going to get hurt by that lunatic. What if Kayden wasn't there? What if he had a gun or something? He could have hurt us both. I mean, I'm now hazardous to be around."

"Stop it. We're in this together."

"What if he hurt you? Maybe I should go away somewhere. I don't want to but I don't know what else to do to keep you and myself safe."

Jade started to cry, and Leo put his hands on her shoulders and stared intently into her eyes.

"Listen to me," He said soberly. "Are you listening?"

"Yes." She sputtered.

He took her face in his hands and gently urged her to focus on him, "The shock is just hitting you. Today has been terrible and scary, and I'm sorry you've had to go through it, but first, you're a survivor. Second, you're tough, even if you don't exactly feel that way right now, and third, I'm here and I'm not going anywhere. We're going to stand and face this together, you understand?"

"Yes, I understand."

They went to sleep with Leo holding her, but Jade had nightmares about being grabbed out of her bed by a monster and she woke up with a start.

Even though Leo had helped to calm Jade down, she was still scared. She shuttered to think of what Joe was capable of. She sat and took a deck of cards out of the coffee table and played a hand of solitaire to calm her nerves and considered her options.

On one hand, she wanted to leave and make sure that no one got hurt by this maniac. It scared her to think of Leo or one of her students getting hurt too, but she had already lost too many people in her life to give up on the life she was making for herself here, and she would not do something stupid and make herself a victim either. There had to be a way to turn the tables on him, but how would she do that? In the movies, beating the bad guy at his own game was fairly easy. In real life, human behavior was much harder to manipulate and predict. There had to be a way to catch him in the act and get rid of him for good. She just had to figure out how to lure him in without getting caught in the trap. It would take a lot of thought and maybe a little bit of luck. Summer break was coming. She didn't know what that would mean to her stalker. Would he take a break or continue to lurk in the shadows. She needed to be extra vigilant and remember that she wasn't taking karate for nothing. She wouldn't be a victim.

Chapter 15:

Inspiration

It is good to love many things, for therein lies the true strength, and whosoever loves much performs much, and can accomplish much, and what is done in love is well done.
-Vincent Van Gogh

Jade finally managed to get a couple of hours of sleep, but she still managed to wake up before Leo, so she decided to do some research. Unfortunately, what she found was nothing she hadn't already figured out the hard way. Although most stalkers have been stalked by a current or former partner, about twenty percent are stalked by a stranger.

Most stalkers are men and they often have a history of previous stalking behavior. Stalking behavior is believed to be motivated by real or perceived rejection. Every state has stalking laws, but the punishment tends to be lax or hard to enforce. Jade decided that she needed to try to find out more about Joe if she was going find a way to end the nightmare.

There was only one way to get more information about him. She would need to call Nick.

"Hi Nick. Did I wake you?"

"You know better than that. How are you?"

"I'm okay. You're sure that Lisa's alright? I worry about her."

"No need. The doctor says that she's doing great. She's worried about you, but she and the baby are fine."

"That's a relief. I miss you both so much."

"We miss you too, but we're glad that you found a job that you love and maybe some nice people to spend time with by the sounds of it."

"Leo's wonderful. The events of yesterday aside, life down here is really good."

"That's awesome, Sweetie!"

"I'm just calling because I was wondering if you could try to reach your friend Al. It would help to get some background on this guy Joe, try to find out what I'm dealing with. You know what I mean."

"I'm ahead of you on that. I emailed Al. Apparently, Joe was in some kind of serious accident. Since Al is deployed, he didn't have a lot of details, but he was going to contact his mother and get back with us when he knew more. That was a few weeks ago. So he is either having trouble reaching his mother, or he's too busy to get back in touch. It could be a combination of both."

"Do you know where his mother lives?"

"I'm not sure. Let me see what I can do. In the meantime, take care of yourself."

"You, too. Hug Lisa for me."

"Will do."

Jade's stomach started to churn, worrying about Joe again. She needed to distract herself, so she decided to go make some blueberry pancakes for breakfast. She put some music on her phone and soon she was absorbed in the task. By the time she was done, Leo still hadn't left the bedroom, so she decided to bring him breakfast in bed.

"That smells great. Come here." Leo said, patting the side of the bed as he sat up.

Jade sat next to him and cut the pancakes up into bite sized pieces and fed him. They took turns feeding each other from the plate, and then Leo picked up the tray and moved it to the floor. He then pinned Jade to the bed, kissing her soundly. His lips were sticky and tasted like blueberries and tea.

"Mmm." Jade moaned.

Leo pulled back and looked at Jade. His gray eyes seemed to sparkle. "I'll show you one of my pieces if you want. Only one, though."

"Really?"

"I'm putting together a series. I have to finish a couple of pieces, but it's going pretty well."

"Show me, please," Jade said as she sat up and pulled him out of bed.

They padded to Leo's studio which had been fashioned out of what had once been a sun porch. The room was filled with easels covered with sheets and canvasses of various sizes leaning against the wall, and a few framed pictures on another wall. The room was cluttered, but was otherwise immaculately clean. Jade stood in the doorway as he walked over to a 4X4 canvas. When he uncovered it, she saw a painting of herself standing with woods in the background. She was smiling and looking out in the distance. Jade was amazed and so flattered that he had painted her. The level of detail was amazing with the way the afternoon sunshine conveyed the glint in her green eyes and struck her hair in the afternoon sunshine. The portrait revealed painstaking textural detail with flecks of endless color. If

Jade was unsure of Leo's feeling for her, it had now all become clear. This painting was painted by someone with such a depth of feeling. Jade realized that she was crying.

Leo had been standing next to the painting, watching Jade's reaction unfold. First was surprise, then happiness, as though remembering the view in the portrait, and finally her eyes began to tear. He waited for her to say something, and when she tried, no sound escaped. Leo stood in front of her and put her hands gently on her shoulders. "Do you like it?"

Her response came out as a moan, "Oh Leo." She put her arms around him and pulled his mouth to hers. When he broke the kiss, she put her head on his chest, breathing in his scent. "Oh my God, I can't believe you painted this. I don't know what to say."

He laughed and played with the ends of her hair. "Nice. You thought I was a hack?"

"Of course not, but Leo—"

"I was inspired."

"Seriously, this should be in a museum or something. You need to show this. I don't know what to say. But Leo, I can't believe you painted me. I'm in awe."

"I paint what moves me." He paused, smiling, "Actually, I hadn't worked on anything in ages, and then you were there."

Jade couldn't stand to be standing so close to Leo without touching him. Her need for him was becoming a physical ache. She started to pull his t-shirt with trembling fingers over his head, then running her hands over his warm, bare chest, and then moved to his pajama pants while she kissed his chest. "Leo…"

"Jade, let's go in the other room. I don't want to start something we can't finish."

She nodded and leaned over to pick up his discarded t-shirt, but before she could stand upright, he had pulled her into a standing position and picked her up to carry her into the bedroom.

"I'm too heavy Leo. You're going to hurt your back!"

"You feel pretty good to me." He said pulling her tight into his chest. "Did I mention how much you inspire me?"

Jade answered a little breathless, "Yeah."

"Well, you're inspiring me again, Jade." Leo said, lowering her onto the bed.

"Really?"

"Let me show you what I mean."

Leo watched Jade sleep. He knew she hadn't slept well the night before, and he hated knowing that she was in danger. He couldn't believe that she hadn't let on about Joe before, but he guessed that she had been hoping that he wasn't a real threat. Unfortunately, she knew differently now. Leo couldn't stand feeling powerless. He knew that even if he dedicated himself to being her constant protector—If Joe was really determined to get to Jade sooner or later, he would find an opportunity, so he did the only thing he could think of to demonstrate how he felt. He showed her his artwork. He wanted her to know that she had inspired him. He just wished he had the guts to say the words he truly wanted to say.

Leo knew he wouldn't be able to hold back much longer though. When he watched Jade looking at the portrait he had painted of her, she had been surprised and impressed with his artistic ability, but Jade was also flattered that she was the subject. What she didn't know yet was that she had served as his muse for the whole series. More importantly, Jade had brought him back to life.

Joe realized that going after Jade in such a public place was a risk, but he had gotten impatient. It had been a big mistake, and now she would be on alert. He would have to find a way to draw her into him next time. The good news was that she was obviously making friends. It was time for him to reach out and touch someone.

Chapter 16:

Turning the Tables

Never forget: This very moment we can change our lives. There never was a moment, and never will be, when we are without the power to alter our destiny.
                                              -Steven Pressfield

Jade knew that Joe was still out there. She still didn't know why he had fixated on her, and she was hoping that Nick might find out more about Joe's background. In the meantime, she planned to be more prepared when he came back around. She decided to talk to someone who was better equipped at self-defense than she. Jade decided that driving during the day by herself might be safer the earlier she went, so she wrote Leo a note and drove herself to the Karate dojo.

"Shihan, do you have a minute?"

Her Karate instructor looked up from his paperwork in the empty dojo and regarded Jade without speaking. She bowed her head in deference to him and sat in a chair across from him.

"I have a problem. There's a man stalking me. It started over the summer when I still lived in Chicago. I moved away in part to get away from him, and then yesterday, he tried to grab me when I was with my students on a field trip."

Jade paused and waited for him to speak. He continued to consider her and then picked up his phone. He dialed a number and when someone answered, he suddenly started speaking rapid fire Japanese, and then abruptly hung up the phone.

Shihan told her, "Wait here," and went back to his paperwork.

A couple of minutes later, the door to the dojo opened and Jade was surprised to see that Leo was standing there, his mouth pulled in a tight line. He didn't say anything but he was clearly angry so she walked over to him.

"Leo—"

"Someone tried to attack you yesterday and you decide to take off on your own? Why?"

"I can't just wait for him to come after me again."

"So we do this together. Don't shut me out, Jade," his voice softened, "Please."

Jade looked at Leo and saw the strain in his face. He had been scared for her. "God Leo, I'm so sorry."

A minute later a car pulled up with several young Japanese men who came into the dojo.

Shihan spoke to Jade, "Karate defense only. Honorable men not attack women. Not studied long. Show ways to defend self from this man. Focus." He considered Leo, and pointed at a chair, "You sit. Watch. Wait."

Jade quickly went to her car to get her karate bag and changed into her gi. She hurried back into the dojo, where she stood, waiting.

Two of the Japanese men exited the dressing room. Jade now recognized them as students who worked with Shihan to help during practice. For the next hour, they demonstrated multiple techniques for countering grabs and holds. She worked on punches and kicks, and by the end of the hour, she was exhausted and sweating from head to toe. Shihan had been watching, directing, but he didn't show much expression. Finally, he looked at Leo and said, "Come."

Leo looked baffled but took off his shoes and socks and walked across the matted floor.

"You watch?"

"Yes."

"Good. You help practice. Keep safe."

"I will. Thank you."

"Maybe you practice?"

"It looks hard, but yes."

He turned and addressed Jade. "Bring back next time. Special rate."

Jade bowed to him and replied, "Osu."

She quickly backed away and went to change into her street clothes.

When she came back out, Shihan was back to his paperwork. Leo took her bag and Jade put her shoes on before they both bowed and left.

"Let's go get some lunch."

Jade left her car in the dojo parking lot and they went to a nearby restaurant. He didn't say anything until they pulled into the parking lot. Leo took the keys out of the truck and turned in the seat.

"Jade, I'm not trying to control you, but please don't just leave me a note again. Talk to me. I trust you, and I hope you trust me to stand by you even if I don't always agree."

"I'm sorry, you're right. I just didn't want you to talk me out of it. I was wrong." She turned her face into his touch and closed her eyes. "Hey, does this count as our first fight?"

He laughed mischievously, "Let's get drive-thru."

They picked up sandwiches and spent the rest of the afternoon in bed.

Chapter 17:

Waiting

*Patience is power, it is not an absence of action;
rather it is timing.*
-Fulton J. Sheen

It had been two weeks since the field trip and Joe's attempted grab, but there had been no sign of him since. Jade continued to stay at Leo's house and had come to regard it as home. They fell into a routine. They drove to work together, ate lunch together, and Leo had even considered beginning to study karate with her, but he wanted to finish his paintings before he did.

Even so, they continued to exercise caution. Jade drove to Karate with Rose, or Leo dropped her off and picked her up. Jade was never alone and even though she took comfort in it, feeling bound to being under constant watch was starting to wear on her. She had gone from being alone most of the time when she lived up north to always being in a group or with Leo at all times.

After Shihan's self-defense lesson, she and Leo continued to practice counter moves. It had been weeks since she had been to the convenience store to get a soda and seen Maddie. Jade hadn't wanted to take a lot of unnecessary trips, so she decided to take a drive while Leo was in his studio and see how she and her son were doing.

Jade knew she shouldn't just leave. Leo wouldn't want her to go out on her own, insisting on going with her, but she didn't want to bother him. Jade would be back before he even missed her, *hopefully*.

"Hey, stranger, where have you been?"

"Long story, I'll tell you all about it later. How's Dakota doing?"

"Better. He still isn't getting along with his math teacher, but he's getting better grades."

"Is he going to have the same math teacher next year?"

"No, thank God! He'll be in junior high and I've heard good things about the teachers there. He's been busy working on his tree house. You should come see it this weekend."

"I would love that. I have your phone number so I'll text you when I know what my plans are."

"Here, let me walk you out." Maddie said, holding the door open. She talked to Jade as she went to stand by Leo's pick up. "Ooh, I like your truck. Is it new?"

"It's not mine, it is Leo's."

"Who's Leo?"

"My friend…well, my boyfriend, actually."

"Wow. You disappear for two weeks and you find a boyfriend. Let me guess, the *'friend'* you went to the hockey game with?"

"Good guess. We work together and I've been staying with him. In fact, I need to get back."

"Okay. I need to get back to work, too but hey, if he has a friend…"

"I will let you know." Jade waved as she got in the truck, "Talk to you later."

Interesting Joe thought when he saw Jade talking to one of the convenience store employees. They appeared to be really friendly too. She might prove to be a very useful person to get to know.

Joe had continued to keep an eye on Jade. It was pretty easy given her set routine. He knew where she lived but he avoided her house. She stayed with that guy. Well he wouldn't always be around, but it would be easier to get to her when she was between work and home.

Of course Joe had to work, but the old man he worked for only cared that he got his jobs done. That gave him plenty of free time, and when he was off, she gave him a sense of purpose. Being a rehab patient had made Joe feel like a child. He had to re-learn to do so many things again and he was tired of people deciding what he could and couldn't have; doctors, therapists, even women tried to tell him what to do. Joe had been discharged months ago, but he still had the headaches.

Jade's rejection was the final straw in a long line of disappointments. No one was going to tell him what he could and couldn't do anymore.

It took him months, but Joe had finally gotten control back of his life by striking out at Diana. It was the first time since the accident he felt in control of his life, and it had felt good, but not nearly as good as he knew it would be to get this stuck up bitch. He would enjoy taking his time with her.

When Jade drove back to Leo's, she knew she was busted. The light in the kitchen was on and he was moving around, probably making something to eat. She felt bad. Jade knew that Leo was only trying to keep her safe but she had started to feel like a caged animal. As much as she cared about Leo, she still needed her own space. She came in the house braced for his anger.

He looked up at her as she walked in the kitchen. "Jade."

"Leo, I know I shouldn't have gone out by myself…"

He raised a hand to stop her from continuing. "Jade, I know this has been hard on you. I don't want to keep you on lockdown like a prisoner. I still think you should be with someone at all times until that lunatic is caught, but I'm not going to get mad at you for going to get a fountain soda or see a friend. I don't want you to feel like you have to sneak away from me."

Jade let a breath. "I'll be glad when I get my life back."

Leo raised his eyebrows, but otherwise didn't respond. After a minute, he turned and said, "I'm going to go back to my studio. Dinner at six?" He walked away without waiting for her to answer.

Hell, when Jade said that she couldn't wait to have the nightmare over with, Leo couldn't help but feel hurt. He was glad to have his painting to distract him. He could understand that Joe stalking her had been scary and having to always have a constant escort was a pain for everyone, but especially for someone who had been so solitary before, but Leo had enjoyed being with her as much as they were. He supposed that at some point he might feel like he needed space since they were working and living together, but he was in love with her.

Leo wasn't sure how Jade felt about him though. She obviously had feelings for him. They had been friends before they became lovers and he protected her when Joe had come after her. He also knew she desired him, yet Leo didn't know if Jade loved him. They had talked about how they felt, and how it all happened so quickly. Leo hadn't expected to feel this nervous ache again after his wife died, but it was so easy to fall in love with Jade. He needed to tell her how he felt.

Jade realized how he must have interpreted her statement as soon as she said it. He must have thought her so ungrateful for all he had done for her. Not everything about the situation was negative. She and Leo were together. Jade probably wouldn't be staying in Leo's house if she hadn't felt threatened, but it had given them an excuse to move in together, and Jade was glad that she had. It was time that she told Leo that.

An hour later, Jade walked into Leo's studio wearing only one of his shirts. "Hi."

"Hi." Leo said, not looking up from his canvas.

"How's it going?"

"Alright, I'll be out in a few minutes." he said, wiping paint on his hands on a rag, but still not looking at her.

"I was going to ask you something if you don't mind."

"Sure."

"Am I in your way here?"

He finally looked at her, "Of course not. Why would you ask me that?"

"Well I was thinking about what I said earlier, about being glad when this nightmare was over. The thing is that's not really true."

He came over to stand in front of her. "What do you mean?"

"It's all been scary as hell at times, but I don't know if I would be living down here and teaching at Nairobi if it weren't for Joe coming after me. I wouldn't have met you, and I don't regret that. I don't regret being here with you. What about you?"

He took her hand and said, "Well I was trying to wait to show you but…"

Leo began uncovering canvases of different sizes, but the one thing they had in common was that she was in all the portraits, all beautifully detailed. "It's me. This is at school standing in the doorway, and this one looks like when we were at the Trail of Tears, the gym after basketball, Me sleeping. They're all of me."

"Yep. Do you like them?"

"Oh my God, Leo, they're amazing. I can't believe it."

"He lowered his head to kiss her but she remained still. She looked up into his eyes as hers filled with unshed tears. "I love you, Leo!"

"I love you, too." Jade reached up around his neck and pulled him to her. Leo reached around and wrapped her up in his arms and then pulled back. "I'm covered in paint. I should wash up."

"I don't care about getting a little paint on my shirt." She laughed, "Luckily, this is your shirt."

Leo was suddenly serious, "Well why don't we go ahead and take it off then."

The next day, Joe waited outside the convenience store where he had seen Jade talking to Maddie. He knew her shift had to be ending soon. Maddie would be very useful at helping plan his long awaited reunion with Jade.

Sure enough, Joe didn't have to wait long. Maddie was all bundled up in her winter coat and not paying attention as she huddled against the mid-December wind. He decided to follow her home, realizing the store had security cameras. Joe kept a safe distance, even though she would have no reason to suspect anyone of following her. She stopped at one house and waited for a moment before running in and coming right back out with a young boy.

"She has a kid," he thought, "Even better." He knew it would be much easier to control her if he threatened her kid.

A minute later, she pulled into another driveway and parked her car. Her son ran in ahead of her while she fumbled with her keys. Joe pulled up into the driveway and pretended to be lost, fumbling with a map until he got onto the porch. He pulled out a knife and told her, "Do exactly what I say or I'll gut him like a deer," before shoving them roughly inside the house.

Nick checked his e-mail and found one from Al marked 'Urgent.'

Nick, I heard from my Mom. She told me that Joe is wanted for questioning by the police. His ex-fiancée and her boyfriend were involved in a hit and run. The witnesses said that a truck hit them, and Joe had access to a lot of different vehicles. The boyfriend's injuries are pretty severe and they aren't sure he's going to make it. The woman is probably going to pull through, but she doesn't remember much.

They don't know anything for certain, but my mother admitted that she had to call the cops on Joe herself for assault. She also told me that Joe was fired from his job because he wrecked a truck and they complained that he had a bad temper. She knows this because Joe was livid over it for a while.

Joe apparently sustained a significant brain injury. The doctors say that his frontal lobe damage mostly affected his personality, but his fiancée finally broke it off when he refused to continue counseling after he got out of the rehab center. She even had an Order of Protection issued against him, but now they can't find him. I know my mother must be worried if she's admitting all of this. He was her baby so she has always tended to make excuses for him. I am so sorry about all of this, Nick. You might want to make sure your friend is okay.

I wish I could help, but there's not much I can do from here.

Al

Nick picked up his cell phone immediately and called Jade. She didn't answer the phone so he called the number he had for Leo, "Hi, Leo? I'm sorry about this, but there's a problem. Do you know where Jade is?"

Leo put the phone on speaker. "She's with me. I have you on speaker."

"What's wrong Nick? Is it Lisa? Are you guys okay?"

"I just heard from Al, Joe's brother. He's wanted for questioning in regarding an attack. They can't locate him."

"What do you mean attack? Someone was hurt? What happened?"

"Apparently Joe's ex and her boyfriend were hit by a truck and Joe wasn't available for questioning, but that's not all…"

Nick told them about his injuries and the incident with his mother and his job.

"Oh my God!"

"Have you seen him?"

"No, not since that afternoon."

"I've been sticking pretty close to her though."

"That's good. I mean, we don't know for sure it was Joe." Nick said, wearily.

"Well the fact that he's in the wind, doesn't look very good."

"That's why I'm calling. Can I just say again that I will never try to fix anyone up."

"Still not your fault, Nick."

"I know, but I still feel awful."

Jade changed the subject. "How is Lisa doing?"

"She's great. The baby's great. The nausea's gone. She's in her second trimester and feeling good. She's out now getting her haircut."

"Well don't tell her, please. I don't want her to worry."

"I don't either, but she'll skin me alive if she finds out I kept this from her."

"Kept what from me? What's going on?" Jade heard in the background.

"Let me call you back, guys."

Joe yanked the phone cord out of the wall.

"I don't care about you. I just want you to call your friend and get her over here, then I'll let you both go." Joe said while duct taping Dakota's wrists together behind his back.

"Please, let my son go. He's just a little boy. I'll do whatever you want, just don't hurt him, please."

"We're going to lock him up."

"The only room that locks is the basement."

He grabbed her arm, "Then lock him in."

"Don't do this. I said I'll do whatever you want."

"I know you will. Just call her and don't get cute."

"Okay. I'll do it."

Maddie called Jade's number and she answered on the second ring. "Hi, Jade. Sorry to bug you again, but Dakota's having trouble with his math assignment. Could you come over and help again? You know he has so much trouble with his calculations."

After a moment, Jade agreed to come over and Maddie hung up.

"Satisfied," Maddie spat.

"I will be. Now, it's time for you to shut up. I have a party to get ready for," he said, just as he punched her in the face; knocking her unconscious.

After Maddie's phone call, Jade's first thought was, "Something's off."

Her voice had sounded normal enough, but Dakota's problems with math weren't calculations. She had a sinking feeling that Joe was behind this but that seemed so crazy. How would he even know that she was friends with Maddie?

But, he had followed her before, so she decided that she had to go there, prepared to face him.

Jade knew that it was past time for her to deal with Joe. She was tired of running. No matter what good had come from her moving south to avoid him, she wanted her life back. Jade wasn't afraid anymore. She didn't know what to tell Leo.

If she told him her suspicions about Joe, he wouldn't let her go. He would insist on calling the police, but what would happen to Maddie and her son? Jade couldn't take the chance. She decided to slip out without telling Leo. Jade decided she would text him when she was on the way. She hoped he would forgive her.

Leo heard the door close. He wasn't sure if she had gone out or was coming back in. He'd crashed out after they had made up, and he'd been up early working on his paintings. He called out to her, "Jade?"

Silence.

He heard his phone buzz indicating a text message. "I went to Maddie's. She needed help with Dakota. I love you."

Leo didn't like it. If Jade was just going over there to help tutor her friend's kid, she would have woken him up before she left. This felt like Jade was sneaking out, but why would she do that. Leo dressed quickly and grabbed his phone, jumped in his truck and called her.

The phone rang a couple of times and went to voicemail. He called again and again, letting it ring a few times and hanging up before the phone went to voicemail again. He hoped she would get tired of hearing her phone and answer it, but she didn't answer it, further confirming his suspicions that she was heading into danger. Leo needed to find Maddie's house. He didn't know where she lived so he went to find someone who did.

The manager of the convenience store didn't want to give him Maddie's address. It was only after he was unable to reach her by phone that he finally relented. Luckily, it was nearby. Leo didn't know what to do as he approached her house. He decided to do something drastic. He needed to create a diversion, so he called 911, "There's a fire at 3120, South Rt. 31."

"What is your name, Sir."

"Leo Blackbird. I was just driving past the house and I saw smoke."

He pulled up nearby and walked through the woods to the back of the house. He saw a young boy running and called out to him. He looked scared and Leo had a hard time catching him.

"Hey little man, what's going on? Are you okay?"

"Who are you?"

"I'm Jade's friend. My name is Leo. Is everything okay?"

"No, there's some crazy man in there with Jade and my mom. He has gun. I'm going to get Mr. Phillips. He'll know what to do."

"You go and be careful."

Leo had a bad feeling as he eased along the back of the house. He couldn't see very well. It was still light out, but the blinds were closed on most of the windows.

He edged up to the house until he reached the kitchen. A woman with dark hair was lying on the floor and appeared to be unconscious. He didn't see Jade or anyone else, but he was now itching to go in and rip this guy's head off. He continued along the side of the house, looking as unobtrusively as possible through the windows. After a couple of minutes, he heard sirens.

Many things happened at once. A blond man appeared at the window and looked out, and he had Jade by the back of her neck. She took his moment of inattention to disengage herself from Joe's grip and shove him head first into the plate glass window. Leo made his presence known and Jade rushed to unlock the door. By the time Leo got into the house, Jade proceeded to kick an unconscious Joe in the hips and ribs. Leo snatched open the door and pulled her away from Joe's prone form, but not before she said one final "Zan shin" and let herself be pulled into Leo's side.

He took off his belt and used it to secure Joe's hands behind his back.

Jade checked on Maddie who was still on the floor, but had started coming to, trying to sit up. "Where's Dakota? Jeez, my head hurts. Find Dakota. Please, Jade."

"We'll find him, I promise. Right now you need to stay down and let the ambulance check you out."

All of a sudden, they heard someone yelling "Mom, mom" just as the police and fire department arrived at the door. Leo started to explain what had transpired as Jade looked after Maddie.

Dakota flew through the door, quickly followed by a handsome dark haired man with a pronounced limp and a military buzz cut. They went right to her side.

"Maddie?"

"Honey," she said reaching up to put her hand on Dakota's concerned face. What are you doing here, Alec?"

"Maddie," Jade interrupted, "I am so sorry you got pulled into this."

Maddie closed her eyes, wincing in pain. "Not your fault. That guy is an asshole. I swear I would kick his ass if I could stand up."

"Don't move. Let them check you out," Alec urged, just as the paramedic eased a stretcher around. It took about an hour, but Maddie was taken to the hospital with Alec while Joe had been taken into custody. Jade had given the police a preliminary report.

"It's over." Leo whispered into her hair. She just held onto him and tried to slow down her breathing.

Joe was taken into custody first by the local police and then by the state troopers. He faced charges of assault, unlawful imprisonment and two counts of attempted murder. Jade learned that he had sustained a brain injury in his car accident. The doctors had tried to get him to continue therapy and take his medication, but they believed he had a disorder called "Intermittent Explosive Disorder," or I.E.D. The fact that he had a brain injury or a psychiatric diagnosis did not excuse what he had done, but it did help explain it.

He had tried to hurt her. He had almost killed his ex-fiancée and her boyfriend and he had terrorized her for months. Nothing would explain any of that away. Jade had to go to the police and be interviewed. Eventually, she would have to go to trial and testify against him, but it was finally over. Her life could now go back to normal, but be irrevocably changed by Joe's actions.

CHAPTER 18:

Normal, or Close Enough

> *It is a great joy to love and be loved.*
> -Laila Gifty Akita

"Did you have a nice winter break?" Mary asked at lunch on the first day back to school.

She looked over and gave Leo a sly smile. "Yeah I did. How about you?"

"It was alright. Busy the whole time, cooking and taking care of sick kids. Do anything interesting?"

Thankfully, someone interrupted before she could answer by talking about her own nightmare holiday illness scenario, so she and Leo were able to avoid further inquiries for the rest of the lunch hour. Just as they were heading back to their classrooms, Jade got a call to go to the office.

"You got a flower delivery." Aleesha told her when she walked in the office with Leo close behind, "And a note."

Jade looked quickly at Leo, and he shrugged.

She accepted the flowers tentatively while Leo took the card.

They took the flowers down to the Jade's classroom and she put the flowers on her desk and sat down as Leo passed her the note without comment. Jade slid her finger to open it and stared at the words on the handwritten page. After a minute, she handed the page to Leo and he read it out loud.

Jade,

I hope you like pink roses. They were your mother's favorite. First of all, I know that I can never make up for not being there all those years, but perhaps I can be a part of your life in some capacity. I want you to know that the biggest regret I have in my life is leaving you. I'm not sure if you will ever speak to me, but there are some things I need to tell you. It has to do with your mother—and before I say this, I want to tell you that nothing is ever one person's fault. Your mother and I had problems. Most of them were my fault. I worked too much and that meant I was away far too much. I neglected my relationship with your mother and after awhile, there wasn't much between us. Your mother was lonely.

She had an affair and as a result, she became pregnant with your sister. Jessie begged me to forgive her. She wanted us to get counseling but I reacted out of hurt and I left. I was a coward. Real men don't run, they stand and fight for what's important. I should have been there for you and your mother. I am sorry I never got to meet your sister Sarah. I am so sorry you had to mourn their loss alone. I am most sorry about the years of your life I missed out on.

I know I don't deserve it, but I hope you will call me sometime.

Love, Dad"

"Are you okay, Jade."

"I didn't see any of that coming but I don't know. I guess I always knew there was something wrong between them, besides the abandonment, of course."

"Well, we can talk about it later."

Jade was blown away by the content of her father's note and just then the bell rung, announcing the end of lunch hour. Jade went to the door to anticipate her students' return as Leo gave her a quick kiss on the cheek. As if reading her mind, he told her, "Don't stress about it. You don't have to do anything until you're ready, if that's what you want. The ball's in your court so you get to decide when. We'll talk tonight, love."

Jade was able to put the unexpected greeting out of her mind after her students entered the class.

On the ride home, Jade spoke about the note first. "When I was a little girl, I used to imagine my father would come back. I had so many different scenarios in my head about what he would be like. He had a really good excuse for leaving, but there were so many things that happened in my life that he was absent for. I can't ever forgive him for that, I just can't."

Leo waited to speak, waiting until he pulled into his driveway. "I don't really know what to say. I have no idea what it would be like to have your father disappear. I can't imagine how much it would hurt."

She got out of the car and walked toward the house. "Yes, but I've been unhappy long enough. I need to let it go."

He put his hand on her shoulder as she put her key in the lock. She pushed the door open and flicked the light on.

Jade walked into the living room just as Leo called out for her to put on a movie and said, "I'll make dinner."

He noticed that he had a voicemail on his phone so he checked his missed calls. It was Ben. He didn't bother to listen to it, but instead, immediately called his father back.

"Dad, you have great timing."

"What do you mean?"

Leo walked into the pantry so he wouldn't be overheard. "Jade heard from her father. She's pretty upset."

"I don't blame her."

"I know. I'm just not sure what to say to her."

"One thing I've learned about women is that they don't want us to fix their problems."

"I know that."

"Yes son, I know that you do, but I also know that when you love someone, it's difficult to stand by and watch them hurt."

"Okay, you're right. So what do I do?"

"Just listen when she needs to talk."

"I can do that, I guess."

"I know you can."

There was silence on the line for a moment, and then Leo spoke. "What's going on?"

"Well, I have news."

Leo noticed that his usually mild mannered father's tone of voice seemed a bit less relaxed than usual. "Is something wrong?"

His father seemed to hesitate a moment before answering. "I'll be closing on the property."

"Really?"

"Yes. It's not far from you, but it will take time to get set up."

"That's great, Dad. It'll be nice to have you close."

"Yes, it will be nice. I've missed you."

"Good. Obviously you know that I'm here if you need me to do anything."

"Yes, I know that. I'm sure I'll need your help at some point."

"When do you think you'll be here? Not that it matters. Just wondering."

"I'm not sure. It'll probably be around the first of June. Perhaps a bit before."

"Dad, I'm not trying to cut you off but I was just about to make dinner. Here, why don't you talk to Jade?"

"I would love to! Put her on."

Leo walked into the living room and handed Jade the phone, "It's my father. Dinner will be ready soon."

"Hey, how are you, Ben?"

"I'm well. How are you?"

"I suppose Leo told you I heard from my father."

"Yes, he mentioned it."

Jade was quiet for a minute so Ben spoke, "You don't have to talk about it if you don't want to."

"I don't mind, but I would rather talk about something else. How is New Life doing? When are you moving? We miss you."

"It is funny that you should mention that."

"This is great! I'll run and get your room set up."

"Jade, take a breath. I'll be there in a couple of weeks. I'll be staying for a bit until I can get my building done."

"We can't wait to have you. We Love you, Ben. We'll be seeing you soon."

Epilogue:

Happily Ever After

"This is happily ever after. It's so much more than that."
-Kiera Cass

Two Weeks Later

"Are you sure everything's okay? You're being a little bit mysterious."

"Everything is fine, dear. All will be revealed later."

"Come on, Ben."

"Don't worry. Tell Leo to take care of you and we'll all go out to dinner someplace nice when I arrive."

"I will. Take care, Ben. Call us later and give us an ETA, alright?"

"See you soon."

Just then Jade heard Leo pull up into the driveway. He had been a little evasive about why he had gone out. Usually they went everywhere together, so Jade was actually a bit relieved for the opportunity to have a couple of hours alone. She had a small matter to take care of that she hadn't wanted Leo around for.

"Hi Honey, I'm home!"

"I'm right here. Did you take care of your errand?"

"Yep," He answered with a sly grin, thinking of the engagement ring he had stashed in his truck. His father was the only one who knew about it.

"Bad news. Your dad had some trouble with his truck. It looks like he's been delayed for a day or two."

"That sucks. Nothing serious, I guess. Otherwise, you would've started mobilizing for a rescue mission." He said smiling and pulling her close.

"Ha, ha. I'm looking forward to seeing him and he's being really mysterious about it."

"I swear, Honey, I wasn't making fun of you."

"Ha!"

"Seriously."

"Well I can't wait for Ben to get here. Do you think he'll like his room? I mean, he's been on his own a long time. I want him to feel comfortable here."

"I'm sure he'll really appreciate it, but he's moving into his own place. He has a business. He has a lot of details to work out before he gets completely moved in and settled."

"I know."

"And just remember that painting the walls the right shade and hanging a dream catcher is not the reason he's going to want to stay. He loves you and he wants to spend more time with us."

"Speaking of that…I have a surprise for you."

"Really, that's a coincidence. I have a surprise for you too. You go first."

She handed him a thick, tie shaped gift box. Leo wasn't wild about ties, but he didn't want to hurt her feelings so he braced himself to appear enthusiastic as he lifted the lid. Inside the box were some folded papers. He pulled them out and read the legal papers with the "Cancellation of Lease" heading. "You're stuck with me now."

All of a sudden he stood abruptly and ran outside to his truck. Jade jumped up and looked out of the kitchen window, trying to guess what had prompted his abrupt departure. She didn't have to wait long because he reappeared at the back door looking a little nervous.

"So here is my news…" He then lowered himself down to his knees in front of her.

Jade gasped and started to cry big fat tears.

He took her hand in his and looked up into her eyes, "Jade Elizabeth Davis, I fell in love with you the first time I saw you standing in your classroom, looking so overwhelmed. You are the most beautiful, kind, and generous woman I have ever known. I can't imagine how I lived my life before you were in it and I don't want to ever try to do it again. I can't promise that our lives together will be perfect, but no matter what fate has in store for us, we can get through it together." He paused and put his arms around her waist, pressing his head into her belly and then looked up, "Marry me?"

"Oh Leo…"

He stood up and smiled, wiping away her tears with his thumbs, "So is that a yes?"

"Yes, Leo, yes," she said, standing on her tiptoes in her stocking feet and kissed him, starting off gently until the kiss became more urgent.

Leo suddenly pulled away, "Hold on a second. We forgot this, where did it go?" He looked down and picked up the small box that had been temporarily discarded. "Oh, here it is. Let's make it official." He said, sliding the ring onto her ring finger.

"It's so beautiful."

"I'm glad you like it. I designed it."

"You did."

"Yep, and you know what else?"

"Does it have to do with celebrating our engagement?"

"No, but that's an awfully good idea."

"Wait, what were you going to say?"

"Well, I found the jeweler that actually made the ring and we got to talking. I guess I'm going to show some of my pieces in a gallery."

"Leo, that's so great. I want to hear all about it and we need to call your Dad." She paused to look at him, and decided to pull his shirt off, "But there are some other pieces I want to talk to you about first."

The End

Acknowledgements

I would never have had the guts to actually finish this were it not for the amazing support of Margreet Asselbergs and Rebecca Sherwin. You believed in me when I didn't believe in myself and helped make this an actual tangible accomplishment. Love you to bits and pieces you amazing ladies.

To Dana Hook, thanks for taking my less than perfect manuscript and helping it flow. I am HAPPY!

To my mother and Bob; thanks for reading draft after draft. I appreciate you always expecting more of me than I have of myself. (Even though it was really annoying when I was in high school. I love you both.)

To my amazing coworkers and friends, you make even the hardest days bearable (especially Doyal and Kaylee) XOXO.

To my students, thank you for being the amazing inspirations that you are.

To the indie reader and writer community (individuals too numerous to list) thanks for showing me that my story had a place to go.

Last but not least, thanks to my honey who has put up with my dreamer ass and lack of housekeeping skills for almost 14 years: I love you!

ABOUT CATHERINE SCOTT

Catherine Scott grew up in the Chicago area but fell in love with the Southern Illinois region while attending university where she studied psychology and special education. She was encouraged to appreciate the outdoors, fine art, film, and books in equal measure from a young age. Catherine has taught the best kids in the world for more than 15 years. She loves reading, travel, old movies, impressionist art, and 80s music. Catherine lives in Kentucky with 3 dogs and the love of her life. She writes romantic suspense novels. "When You Least Expect It" is the first novel in her Great Expectations series.

You can find me here:

https://www.facebook.com/pages/Catherine-Scott-Author/709578675746339

https://twitter.com/cscott_author

Made in the USA
Charleston, SC
03 March 2016